BROKEN ON
THE INSIDE

Broken on
the Inside

by

Phil Sloman

Black Shuck Books
www.BlackShuckBooks.co.uk

Discomfort Food was originally published in *Chip Shop Horrors* (KnightWatch Press, 2015)
The Man Who Fed the Foxes was originally published in *Bones III* (James Ward Kirk Publishing, 2014)
There Was an Old Man was originally published in *Phobophobias* (Western Legends Publishing, 2014)
Virtually Famous was originally published in *Imposter Syndrome* (Dark Minds Press, 2017)

Cover design & internal layout © WHITEspace 2019

First published in the UK by Black Shuck Books, 2018

978-1-913038-11-3

Broken on
the Inside

"What did the doctor say, Kira love?"

The words were bitingly familiar by now. A routine had grown where none should ever have existed. Each time her mother's greeting would echo down the hallway as the front door closed behind Kira. Her mother Constance – Connie to her friends – would be waiting in the kitchen. A cup of coffee beside her and a cigarette balanced delicately between her second and middle finger, with another fag poking from the packet ready to go. And Kira would pause to hang up her coat or remove her shades or shake out her umbrella or whatever practice the time of the year suggested. Always something to give her a few more seconds to her own thoughts before facing the gentle questioning of her mother.

There was a tightness to Kira's skin as it

adjusted to the change in temperature; constricting, reacting to the warmth of the hallway in sharp contrast to the frost touched streets of south London. Others would have missed it but these were the things she noticed. Always. She had been like that ever since she was a little girl. Sensitive. In tune with the variations in her body. A hyperawareness to the biological abnormalities which arose within her far too frequently.

"Let me get my coat off first, Mum, then I'll sit down and tell you." Then, almost as an afterthought, "Hope you've got a brew on in there."

Kira thought about what she was going to say to her mother. How she was going to broach the subject without seemingly asking for permission. Hell, she was twenty-two after all and a long way from needing to hang from her mother's apron strings for anything. Well, most things. After the dizzying freedom of university she had fallen back to earth with a sharp thud. The world was meant to be her oyster. Promises throughout her life of studying hard and that being the route to reaping the rewards she was due. And she had worked hard. Really bloody hard. Studying in the evenings when her friends would be out down the student union. Taking on additional assignments to expand her learning. And she'd done well. Very well. Very fucking well indeed. Almost scraping a first but not quite. "That's a shame, love, but well done anyway." She still remembered the slight disappointment in her mother's voice, that partial drop in tone before the rise at the end.

Her mother had said the same thing when the doctors had said she would need further tests for her problems. "That's a shame."

Her *problems* – her mother always used that word when speaking about Kira's health – had started soon after she had moved back home. The symptoms had been marginal to begin with. Unexplained pains; nothing more than dull aches which came and went. A general feeling of lethargy. She had ignored it all at the time.

"Any chance of a biscuit, too?" Kira's voice echoed down the narrow corridor.

Kira's *problems* had only developed further from there. She would wake in the night wracked with sweat and doubled over with stomach cramps. Daytime would bring nausea and dizziness. She was constantly washed out.

Flu, her mother had suggested, but it didn't pass.

Her GP had been of little to no use at all, struggling to find anything wrong with her. She had been referred on to the hospital, where doctors with fancy-sounding job titles had undertaken test upon test.

Kira's nose wrinkled as she entered the kitchen. A thin layer of smoke filled the room, even with the window open. The ashtray on the table was filled with discarded butts. Her mother had a fresh cigarette on the go as she paced the kitchen, arms partially folded across her chest. Generally she only smoked a packet a day – it was on days like today when she chained them.

Connie made an effort to smile, her lips parting to reveal yellowed teeth, but the sense of comfort and ease never made its way to her eyes.

"So, how did it go, love?"

How did it go? Really fucking well, Mum. Really fucking well. But there's something you're not going to like. And you're going to give me a hard time. But I don't care. I really don't fucking care. I just want to be better, Mum. I want to be normal again.

She wanted to blurt all that out and more. Instead she opted for caution.

"Can we sit down, Mum?"

"Right, sure." Connie's smile vanished, her voice hesitant, her speech stilted. "Your, er, your drink's there, love."

Chairs scraped on cheap tiles as they both took a seat facing the other across the small kitchen table. Kira pulled her drink towards her, clocking the ginger biscuit nestled in the saucer.

"Thanks, Mum."

Kira cradled the cup in her hands, relishing the warmth, enjoying the tingling sensation running through her fingers and the distraction it brought. Steam rose from her tea to mingle with the low lying smoke. She thought of how she was going to break things to her mother, how she could let her know the outcome without the inevitable histrionics. The histrionics which had made her stop Connie from accompanying her to any further medical appointments.

"Mum…" She paused, seeing the mask of uncertainty set on her mother's face as Connie waited for the news; desperate to know whether there was a cure for her daughter. Her baby girl. Kira sat silent with the clock on the wall counting off each eternal second, one after the other. Ash dropped from Connie's cigarette onto the table top.

"Oh God, love, are you going to tell me or not? What did they say?"

Kira thought back to her conversation with Dr Secombe that morning. And to all the other conversations she had had with him. She had been referred to Secombe shortly after the decision to stop her mother coming to any appointments had been taken. A decision which had provoked a spate of arguments at home; yet that was when things began to get better. Her mother would undoubtedly have interfered – asking question after irritating question, making decisions on Kira's behalf, stopping her going down this route. A route which offered her hope. A route where Dr Secombe had presented her with a solution. With a chance at happiness.

"It's okay, Mum. It's good news."

Good news, Mum. See. Nothing to worry about. Please be happy for me. Please don't ask questions.

Connie breathed a sigh of relief, a thin drift of smoke spilling from her lips. She reached across the table and grabbed her daughter's hand. There was a renewed fire in her eyes which had lain dormant for months.

"Have…have they found a cure?"

A cure. Connie was almost afraid to say the word, as if speaking it out loud would scare it away back into the darkness. She gripped Kira's hand tighter.

"It's too early to say for definite but they think so."

I know so.

"Really?"

"Yes, but…"

"But? But what?"

"Let me finish, Mum." Kira slipped from her mother's grip and sipped at her drink, the tea still kettle hot, buying a few precious seconds while the news was still hers to give. "They want to try something new. It's a prototype of sorts."

"A prototype?"

That tone. Always that tone. The underlying sentiment. That's a shame, love.

"Don't be like that, Mum. Dr Secombe is very enthusiastic about the procedure. They pioneered it in America. He says the results are one hundred percent effective."

"Pioneered what? And on who? Don't tell me it was tested on rats or something."

"On people, Mum. Real life people like you

and me. People who have recovered, who've gone on to lead happy normal lives! Aren't you excited, Mum? I'm excited. Please, Mum. Please. Please tell me you're excited."

Connie stubbed out her cigarette. A smear of grey streaked across the bottom of the ashtray. Another cigarette was instinctively plucked from the open packet.

"Aren't you going to say anything, Mum? I thought you'd be pleased."

The lines on Connie's face became more apparent in the flare of her lighter. She took a drag on her cigarette, savouring the taste before exhaling.

"I am pleased. I just..." Pause. Inhale. Hold. Exhale. "I just don't know what to think really."

Kira had been the same when having her initial conversation with Dr Secombe. Unsure. It all sounded like something from a science fiction book, one of those ones where technology offered the solution but there was always a payoff. She had read about nanotechnology in the papers, snippets scanned briefly as she flicked through the pages trying to find anything of interest to read among the advertising and the gossip. She hadn't imagined it would become part of her life. It had all seemed years away – possibly even a generation or two before it would be ready for public use. Yet there he was offering her that very solution. Dr Secombe made it sound so feasible, like an opportunity she should grasp there and then. Like the answer to all her prayers. And she had prayed so much over the preceding months.

"How about being happy for me, Mum. That would be a start, because I'm going through with it whether you like it or not."

~

Kira awoke to find sunlight streaming in through the curtains of her hospital suite. Across the room, someone had put a yellow bunch of flowers into a vase on the corner table. She thought they might be a type of lily but wasn't sure – either way they added a welcome flash of colour into the otherwise white room. An ornate jug of water sat on her bedside table, its swan neck bending elegantly as it caught the light. She licked her lips, scraping at the covering of fur on her tongue which caught on the edge of her teeth. She could taste pear drops, though she couldn't recall having eaten any, and the inside of her mouth felt dry. That part was understandable. She had needed to be nil by mouth for twenty-four hours before the procedure.

Oh God, the procedure.

Long desperate fingers clawed at her top as she scrabbled to assess the damage. The large buttons popped free with ease, the soft cotton fabric offering little resistance. The tips of her fingers raced across the dark smoothness of her skin, hunting for the point of entry.

Had everything gone as planned? Where were the doctors and nurses? Was it a good sign that they had left her alone in the room or did it mean something different?

She explored the landscape of her body, the raised contours of her ribs giving way to the flat drift of her stomach as her fingers ventured towards her navel. It was waiting for her there, located to the left of her belly button. The incision. There was an oily sheen to her skin where they had prepared her for surgery. She might have missed the cut itself had she not been looking for it. The entry point was barely a centimetre across, the precision remarkable, testimony to the surgical skills of the clinician.

Kira prodded at the snick. Tentatively at first, probing gently. Then more aggressively. Testing it, assessing the damage, investigating what had been done to her. Relief washed over her with each passing second. It was incredible. No bruising, or none she could feel. Whatever stitching they had used was nigh on invisible. She had been worried about a scar but from what she could tell that seemed unlikely.

Oh my God, this is amazing!

But that's on the outside – the cosmetic part. What about the inside? Nothing felt different yet but how would she tell what was new?

Her thoughts were broken by an inquiring knock on the door to her suite.

"Miss Jones?"

The voice was male. Cautious. Familiar yet she couldn't quite place it.

"Miss Jones? Kira? Are you awake?"

"Um, yes. I'm awake. Who is it?"

"It's Dr Secombe. May I come in? Are you decent?"

Decent? Who used language like that nowadays?

"I've got clothes on, if that's what you mean."

"Excellent, excellent."

The door swung open with ease to reveal the portly figure of the man who had promised to transform her life. Small round glasses perched on the bridge of his nose, the thin wire frames wrapped around the side of his head. The lack of hair on his scalp was made up for by a pepper-coated beard which hid facial scarring from his youth.

He walked to the end of the bed and retrieved the patient records from their holder. Several pages of notes were held in place on a plastic clipboard, with Kira's name written on the top in an ineligible black scrawl. Beneath were details of blood pressures, diet, medications received and so on and so forth. Dr Secombe grunted his satisfaction as he flicked through the sheets of paper.

"Wonderful. Yes. Exactly as we hoped for." The words were mumbled under his breath, almost as if he had forgotten his patient was there. Catching himself, he looked up. "And I must say, you are looking exceptionally well, Kira. How are you feeling?"

"Good. I guess."

"Good, good." Dr Secombe had returned his gaze to the notes. "Did you sleep well?"

"Yes, um, I think so. To tell you the truth I don't remember much about getting here."

Secombe put the notes back in their holder.

"Do you mind if I pull up a chair?"

He did so anyway without waiting for Kira's response. His backside partially hung over the edge as he seated himself, but it didn't seem to bother him.

"Firstly, let me reassure you that everything went as well as could be."

"As well as could be?" There was a note of caution in Kira's voice. Had things gone wrong after all? Was this the conversation to let her down gently? To tell her all her hopes and dreams were about to come crashing down?

"Well, actually they went pretty darned well to be fair. Almost perfect, I would say."

Kira could feel a weight lift from her chest.

"In fact, if everything checks out over the next few days then I reckon we can look to send you back home by the weekend. How does that sound?"

"Oh doctor, that sounds amazing." And then the shadow of doubt crossed Kira's mind. A shadow which had been with her for years. The one which always told her she couldn't have nice things. The one which focused on the pitfalls and the failures. The one which said things like *'That's a shame.'* "But how do I know it's working? I can't feel anything inside of me."

Dr Secombe smiled a broad smile. The smile of a man knowing he is in full control of a situation, enjoying the drip feed of information and the power it gave him.

"We need to turn it on."

Kira looked at him blankly. From all their conversations she had assumed that it would almost be instantaneous, in the same way a pacemaker was simply expected to perform from the off.

"It's quite simple really. When you are ready we'll give one flick of the switch, so to speak, and then Pam will start up. Didn't want to startle you with her before we knew you were all fine."

"Pam?"

"Patient artificial monitoring system. We like to call it Pam for short. You say the word and we'll fire her up." Secombe put a hand on Kira's arm. "But there's a few things we need to go through first."

~

Kira jumped the first time Pam spoke to her.

Pam's voice was more human than she had expected, almost like a thought drifting through her mind rather than the disembodied mechanical tone she had expected. It had the same south London lilt she was used to hearing every day, a melting pot of accents which held their own rhythm. Dr Secombe had spoken with her about this, explaining how her mind would reconstruct the cadence and tone of Pam's words into something more familiar. More welcoming. It was all designed to make the integration as streamlined as possible. Secombe had described how in the early trials the voices had been along the lines of HAL 9000. It was a reference Kira didn't properly understand beyond Secombe's suggestion of a sense of creepiness. Test subjects had quit the programme, he'd said, citing heightened levels of paranoia but that had all been ironed out now. As he spoke, his eyes had been as reassuring as his words, a paternal nature to the way he interacted with her, a sense of trust and warmth. The consummate bedside manner.

Mild dehydration. Perhaps you would like a glass of water, Kira?

Those had been Pam's first words.

Kira wasn't sure what she had expected. Maybe something more devastating. Less inauspicious. Something along the lines of *major internal organ failure*. Or *heart attack imminent*. Perhaps *cancerous cells detected*. Definitely nothing as simple and understated as this. Or as polite.

"Erm, thank you. Pam." The use of Pam's name was an afterthought. A cautious approach to a stranger. A stranger with responsibility for her health. A stranger who was inside her.

You are most welcome, Kira.

Kira poured herself a glass of water from the jug on the bedside table. The water was at room temperature yet still refreshing. Kira took another sip, waiting for some response from Pam. Is that what happened? You tried to fix the problem and she – Kira corrected herself – *it* would let you know the outcome?

"Pam?" Kira's voice was tentative, the novelty of speaking out loud in an empty room making her feel self-conscious even though there was no one else there to judge her. But what if someone came in? Would they think she was crazy or was this the norm around here? Dr Secombe had said

Pam picked up auditory cues, using the body's own hearing mechanism to translate external prompts, but could she simply think her words and Pam would pick them up? He had never said either way.

Pam, can you hear me?

Nothing.

Then...

Beginning full diagnostic report. Please wait.

And as Pam read out the issues and the solutions she had put in place Kira knew this was the beginning of something good.

~

"So, is it talking to you right now?"

"For the hundredth time, Mum, it only speaks to me when something's wrong."

It had been a week since Kira had been discharged from the clinic. In many ways it had been the best week she had had in recent memory. Gone were the cramps in the night and the need to wash yet another set of sweat-stained bedding. For that alone she was grateful. Along with that there were no more bouts of daytime nausea. No more unexplained reasons for cancelling on friends at the last minute – a friendship group which had dwindled as her illness worsened – and a freedom to simply live, to go out into the wider world beyond the one which existed between her mother's house and the varying clinical appointments.

Kira hadn't realised until now just how much her condition had impacted her life. How much it had changed her as an individual. Reducing a confident vivacious young woman into a wreck of humanity – a wreck she struggled to recognise when she looked in the mirror. But all that was in the past now. From here on in she was going to grab life and squeeze every last ounce of fun from it. If her mother would let her, that was.

"But how does it know if something is wrong?" Connie raised up a dismissive hand to stop Kira interrupting. "I know, I know. You've told me a hundred times. But humour your mother, would you. I'm worried about you, that's all. What kind of a mother would I be if I didn't worry about my little baby girl?"

Kira sighed inwardly.

"It just knows, Mum. You have to trust it. I mean, look at how great I look now. I feel alive, Mum. I feel like me again."

Connie looked at her daughter, reaching into her own sweater pocket for the packet of cigarettes stashed inside at the same time. The familiarity of the packet in her hand was a comfort in and of itself.

"But what if it breaks down? What then?"

That's a shame, love.

"But it won't. They've tested it over and over again, Mum. It's not going to break down."

"That's what they said about the Titanic."

"What?"

"They said it wouldn't sink and look what happened there."

"It's got nothing to do with the Titanic. Or anything else for that matter."

"Well it's still not right, having something like that stuck inside you. You should have at least let me come along to the clinic with you."

"And what good would that have done? What difference would it have made?"

"Perhaps I could have had a word with this Dr Slocombe of yours."

"Secombe, Mum. It's Dr Secombe."

"Well, whatever he's called, I'm still not sure that I trust what he's done."

"Mum, please!" The words were more forceful

than Kira had meant. She didn't care. "I've told you over and over again. Dr Secombe is an expert in all of this. One of the leading people in the country.

"And this Dr Secombe knows better than your own mother then, does he?"

"Actually yes, Mum. Yes he fucking does."

Connie took a step back. The words were a metaphorical slap across the face.

"I think you should watch your language, young lady." Connie fumbled a cigarette from the packet. "That's if you want to stay living under this roof."

"Mum! Really? I'm not fourteen you know."

"I don't care. This is my house and I will not be spoken to like that. Do you hear me?"

Kira pursed her lips, looking out the window, to the floor, the ceiling, anywhere but her mother.

"I said did you hear me, young lady?"

A plume of smoke escaped Connie's lips as she sparked up her cigarette.

"Yes, I heard you." The sense of being a teenager again reared its head for one more time than Kira cared to remember. "Look, Mum, I'm sorry I swore but this is important to me even if it isn't to you."

Connie's face thundered.

"It's not only the swearing, Kira. It's your whole attitude of late..."

Airborne carcinogens detected.

Pam's voice caught Kira unawares.

"...and how dare you say it's not important to me. If you don't start appreciating what I've sacrificed for you over the years then perhaps..."

Perhaps you should leave the immediate area, Kira.

Kira looked at the cigarette in Connie's hand. Already there was a grey stretch of ash forming along the length of the fag, waiting to be tapped into the sink where it would be washed away.

"Mum."

"What, Kira?" The response was curt, punctuated with another drag on her cigarette.

"Please could you put out your fag?" Her words were tentative. Her mum had always smoked. Always. Other people spoke about quitting but never her. It helped with her nerves – kept her steady, as she liked to say. Kira had seen the reaction people got in pubs or in the supermarket if anyone challenged her mother when she lit up.

"Pardon?"

"I said," Kira spoke up, "please can you put out your fag. For me. Pam says…"

"Pam says what?"

Kira looked to her feet, not wanting to put blame for her health at her mother, not even the slightest hint of complicity. The silence said everything.

"So I can't smoke in my own home now!"

"Of course you can, Mum. Just not around me."

"Fine!" Connie mashed her cigarette into the laminated countertop. The surface blistered where the red hot tip contacted with the plastic, before the white and orange paper folded on top of itself to contain the damage. "I'll be down The Crown if you need me. You and Pam can entertain yourselves here on your own."

The front door had opened and slammed before Kira could think of what to say.

~

Excessive alcohol intake. Perhaps you should switch to water, Kira.

Kira ignored the voice inside her head and ordered two more brandy and cokes. Pam could lecture her all she wanted, it didn't matter.

Tonight was about getting completely and utterly shitfaced.

The music in the club wasn't what she was after but she didn't really care. Kira was glad to be out and away from the constant questioning of her mother. She had phoned her friend Jamila – one of the few friends who were still there for her – on the spur of the moment. "I need to get out, blow the cobwebs away. Please." It had been the right call.

She was having fun for the first time in a long while and it felt good.

"What do you think of the barman?" A splash of liquid spilt from the glasses as Kira put them down on the table. "He said for you to go up next time and he'd sort you out."

"I hope you told him to go fuck himself!"

"No. I gave him your number."

"You didn't! Christ, how could you? I'm going to..." Jamila stopped as she saw Kira laughing at her from across the table. "Yeah, funny. Very fucking funny! Really fucking mature."

"Your face!" Kira said pointing.

"Don't you go expecting any more drinks from me later, okay."

"Jay!"

"Not so funny now, is it?"

"Seriously?"

Jamila smiled.

"Of course not, babe. You've been hiding away for far too long. What kind of cheapskate do you take me for? We're sisters, yeah."

Kira felt a warmth inside her which she had forgotten even existed.

"Sisters!" She raised her glass and Jamila did the same.

"Sisters forever!"

Jamila jolted forward before she could take a drink. Liquid sloshed from her glass on to Kira.

"Hey, watch it, dickhead!" Jamila shouted over her shoulder into thin air. Whoever had barged her was long gone into the throng of bodies. "Are you okay, hon? I didn't get too much on you, did I?"

Kira brushed her top down. Small droplets of liquid soaked into the dark fabric.

"It'll wash out. Don't worry."

"Sure?"

"Sure."

"Okay, that's...oh, shit, don't look."

"What?"

"There, over there. That guy....no, I said don't look. He keeps looking over at you."

"Of course there is. It's a club. Guys are always staring."

"Yeah, but this one's cute."

Kira looked to Jamila for any signs of deception, the darkness of the club making her face hard to read. And then realisation dawned. "Really? You mean properly cute? Where?"

Jamila nodded, raising a pencilled eyebrow as she did so, indicating a direction somewhere behind Kira, across the other side of the dancefloor.

"Behind you. But don't look!"

Jamila sighed as Kira turned around, looking across and beyond the gyrating bodies on the dance floor.

"I said don't look!" Jamila grabbed Kira's wrist to bring her attention back to their table. "Oh my God, you are so bad."

"What?" Kira sipped her drink, giving Jamila a knowing wink as she ignored a further reprimand from Pam. "Did I do something wrong?"

Jamila laughed. "You know you did. You're meant to play things cool. Remember."

"Right." Kira took another sip. Red lipstick marked the rim of her glass. "So which one was he?"

"The one checking you out?"

"Yeah."

"Tall, smooth head, works out. You know, ugly."

"Ugly? I thought you said he was cute."

"Nah, he's ugly. In a kind of model way. If that's your thing."

They both laughed.

"Well in that case, I might just go over to talk to him."

"I don't think you'll need to."

"What do you mean?"

Before Jamila could answer, Kira felt a hand on her shoulder.

"Hi, there. I'm Tito. Perhaps I could buy you a drink?"

~

The cab drive back to Kira's had been intense. They'd kissed passionately, her hands running over the tautness of his stomach, her fingers feeling the contours, exploring, not quite bold enough to venture higher or lower while they had the driver as an audience. In turn he had cradled the curve of her backside in his hands, drawing her into him as much as he dared.

They had stumbled into Kira's house. A raised finger to Kira's lips told Tito to be quiet. Her mother was probably home. Probably. She hadn't returned by the time Kira had left. She had most likely stayed until closing time down at The Crown and would be sleeping off the booze now in her room. Dead to the world. But even still.

Their movements were cautious. Taking the stairs one step at a time, Kira led the way, holding Tito's hand as if she were guiding a child. At one point she paused, the creak of a floorboard sounding like an earth tremor in the stillness of the house. Tito almost crashed into the back of her causing her to laugh and giggle. She shouldn't be doing this at twenty-two. Sneaking around like some guilty teenager. But it didn't matter – what mattered was the here and now.

And now they were in her bedroom.

She flung her coat and handbag to the floor even as his lips found hers again. Kissing they fell on to the bed. Lips moved to necks. Delicately brushing skin, savouring each other, both reacting to the sounds the other one made. Fingers scrabbled at clothing. Bodies parted to remove layers of clothing, only to reunite. Skin on skin. Feeling the heat of each other. Lips exploring again. Fingers doing the same. Tongues tasting. Seconds ticking into minutes. Losing themselves in each other. Pulses quickening. And then a pause.

Kira's hand on Tito's chest. Holding him back. The rhythm of his heart beating hard and fast against her palm.

"Wait! Do," her words were breathy, "do you have protection?

"Yes." He kissed her, prolonging the anticipation. "In my wallet."

"Get it."

He didn't move

"Get it. Please."

And then he was off her. Hunting desperately for his trousers. Finding them. Then his hands seemed suddenly too big to reach inside the pocket, only for the wallet to appear at last. Kira lay there in frustrated anticipation, drinking him in with her eyes, admiring his body as he fumbled the silver wrapper from within the leather. Watching as he tore open the packet before rolling the condom along his cock.

And then they were together again. Kissing. Licking. Fucking.

"Do you like that, baby?"

Tito was stroking her hair with his hand, his hips moving in time with hers, a gentle rise and fall as they became used to each other.

"Yeah, it's good. Keep going."

The cautious enquiry and encouragement of new lovers.

Danger. Foreign body detected.

Pam's voice. That south London lilt when she didn't want it.

"How about this?"

He adjusted his legs, changing the angle, waiting for a reaction.

Danger. Internal damage detected. Danger.

Except the south London lilt had morphed now. Something even closer to home. Something which startled her.

"Baby?" Tito's voice was uncertain. Kira's face distorting in front of him, changing from pleasure to terror. Her movements now out of synch with Tito's. He slowed, unsure whether to continue, yet unwilling to stop.

Danger! Danger!

Her mother's voice was unmistakeable. Shouting inside her head. Telling her she couldn't do what she wanted to do. Even here and now she couldn't let Kira have a moment of joy.

"Get out! Get out! Get out of my fucking head!"

"You what?"

Kira pushed him off her, pulling herself away from him. Leaving him prone.

That's a shame, love.

"Get out! Get out! Get out!" she screamed.

"Well fuck you, you crazy bitch!"

Kira was hard up against the headboard, her knees pulled up to her chest, her hands beating at the sides of her head, trying to force the voice – her mother – out of her. Tito ignored her, gathering up his clothing, picking up items strewn across the bedroom, struggling to pull up his underwear and jeans. And all the time Kira kept screaming her litany of anguish.

"You're mental, you know that. Fucking mental." The words were flung at her as Tito stormed from her bedroom. Pausing to leave that one last parting shot. Barging past Connie, who stood in the doorway bleary eyed and dishevelled.

And that was the last time Kira ever heard from Tito.

~

Breakfast was uncomfortable the next morning.

Connie had tried to broach the subject of the night before. To set some ground rules. But Kira had refused to engage. So here they were, mother and daughter sitting in silence.

Connie got up.

"I'll make you eggs. You like a nice egg, love."

Kira grunted. The same worries repeated over and over in her head. Again and again. All she could think about was last night and the voice. It must have been the alcohol. She hadn't drunk that much in a long time. Not since university. Thinking back she couldn't be sure it had been her mother's voice. But even if it wasn't then what did the words mean for her and the rest of her life? Did it mean she couldn't go out drinking with her friends again without being told off like a naughty child? And what if she met another bloke that she liked? What then? Was this it? No more sex? Or could she get used to it and ignore things, find a way to override it? Dr Secombe had never mentioned an off switch. Pam was meant to be powered 24/7, using small surges of energy from Kira's body to keep her –

it, to keep *it* – running, the nanotechnology self-healing in the same way it helped to heal her. And what if she wanted to have children? Would it see those as a threat within her? An unwanted foreign body for the nanotechnology to attack and remove?

"There's your egg, love. Soft boiled just as you like it."

Kira looked up, realising how lost she was in her own world, how time was slipping by her. She would have to speak to Dr Secombe – ask him for his advice, see if any of the other patients had experienced anything similar. What if she had a faulty model? Even after all the testing and all the reassurances from Dr Secombe, what if she was unlucky in life once again?

She picked up her cutlery out of habit, cracking the side of the egg with her knife before using it to remove the top. The yolk inside was nice and runny in the way only her mother could ever make it. The albumen was mostly solid except around the centre where it had the soft gelatinous texture of a jellyfish. That didn't matter. She wouldn't notice if she mixed it in with the yolk. She could eat quickly and then be gone. Kira dipped her teaspoon in and took a mouthful.

Caution. Risk of salmonella. Do not swallow.

Kira spat the food back onto her plate, a saliva-flecked spray of egg coating the plate and the surrounding table surface. The voice was her mother's, but her mother was sitting across from her, mouth open aghast in silent reprimand. And in the globules of rejected egg lay the essence of Kira's future. Everything to be questioned. No more risks to be taken. No more fun to be had. A life full of spat out opportunities and the loneliness which came with it.

Kira ran crying from the kitchen and then from the house and then into the street and the pouring rain.

~

Kira staggered haphazardly along the south London streets, hair plastered to her scalp as the rains fell, hands cupping her ears and cradling her skull in a futile attempt to stop the admonishments. Feeling like she wanted to mentally vomit the thoughts which were dogging her every step.

Get out of the wet. You'll catch your death from cold.

Don't cross against the red man. Follow the Green Cross Code.

Don't step on a crack, it'll break your mother's back.

On and on and on. The internal and external dangers mingling now in a cacophony of well-meaning and good intentions.

She went to phone Jamila, to phone Dr Secombe, to phone anyone who might help her. Except the phone felt hot in her hands and the voice continued. Her mother scalding her from within and afar.

Are those things safe? Don't they give off radiation poisoning? Won't you fry your brain, love? That's a shame, love. That's a shame.

Kira screamed. People stared. The phone skidded across the road as she threw it away from her, shattering into a thousand pieces as it was repeatedly crushed under the oncoming traffic.

You're making a scene, love. What will the neighbours say, love?

Kira didn't care. She just wanted the voice to stop.

~

"Kira, I can't make it stop. Not here. Not now. I have other patients I need to treat."

"Then when?"

Pity had filled Dr Secombe's eyes as he looked at his patient.

"Tomorrow. Come back tomorrow. We can get everything fixed then." He looked at his watch. "Just not today."

That had been a couple of hours ago. Kira's route had wound through London until she arrived at the clinic. Dr Secombe had refused to see her at first; he was in with another patient. That was fine, she could wait. She wished she hadn't.

The one man she thought could fix everything with the flick of a switch had let her down. Yes, tomorrow would come but what about today? What about this evening? What about tonight? Her mother – no, Pam, not her mother, Pam – was in her head every other minute. A person coughing as Kira walked by: *Caution*. A dog running past her in the street: *Caution*. Building works: *Caution, caution, motherfucking caution!*

And now she was standing outside the front door to her house with fresh tears rolling down her face and she didn't know how to make them stop. Too scared to go in to talk to her mother about last night, yet too scared to stay out in the street.

Connie made the decision for her.

"Come in, love. You'll catch your death out there."

Kira thought it was Pam at first. It took her a moment to realise her mother was standing in the doorway with open arms.

"I'm scared, Mum. I'm really fucking scared." Snot and mucus distorted her words. Kira flinched as her mother put her arms around her, pulling Kira into her body, holding her tight to keep the pain of the world away. They stood like that for several minutes, Connie's clothes dampening as she cuddled Kira closer.

"Shall we go inside?"

Kira looked up into the warmth of her mother's face and nodded.

Connie led Kira into the kitchen, guiding her to take a seat.

"I'll get you a cuppa, love. Then we'll talk."

Kira nodded then changed her mind as warnings about scalding water shrieked within her head.

"A cold drink, please. In a cup."

Good girl. No broken glass to worry about.

Her mother's jaw clenched, hidden away from Kira's view, then relaxed again.

"Of course, love."

The mug slopped water as Connie placed it on the table.

"I'll get us some cake to go with it."

"Yes, cake. Cake would be nice." *Choking hazard.* "A small piece. Please."

That clench again.

Crockery rattled on the table as Connie set out two plates. A louder thud as a chocolate cake was placed centre stage. Then the sound of a drawer sliding open and shutting.

Danger! Danger! Danger!

Kira shied backwards, retreating into the curve of her chair, her knees drawing up, her arms folding loosely then tightening. Trying to act normal. Trying to be her again. Failing.

There was a chink which focused her attention as the knife cut through the dark layers of cake, all the way down to the glazed rim of the plate. Another chink. Then a scrape and a gentle imperceptible thud as the slice was presented to Kira. Repetition and then a second slice placed

in front of Connie this time. The knife itself –
the danger, the threat – was left sticking
prominently from the top of the remaining cake
like some badly imagined Arthurian legend. Kira
tried to ignore it.

"Kira?" Her mother's voice was soft in the way
Kira remembered it as a child, that protective
cotton wool which would make everything right
again. "I'm worried about you."

Get rid of the knife, Kira.

Kira ignored Pam.

"I'm fine, Mum."

Connie raised an eyebrow.

"No, you're not. Look at you. You look like
you've been..." Connie paused, regaining herself,
slowing her words and softening her tone again.
"Kira, if you can't admit it to me then at least
admit it to yourself. Something is really wrong
here."

"Mum, it's fine. Really."

"Really? Everything's fine? You're sure of
that?"

"Yes, Mum. Really. I've an appointment with
Dr Secombe tomorrow. He's going to make
everything right again. It's just a minor
adjustment."

Connie folded her arms across her chest.

"That's right. Your Dr Secombe. Well as far as I can see this is all his fault. His and yours. You should have listened to me sooner, love."

She doesn't care about you, Kira. Don't listen to her. She's the threat. She's the one putting you in danger.

"I know what I'm doing, Mum."

"No, Kira, I really don't think you do. And yet again I'm going to have to pick up the pieces for you and sort things out with this doctor of yours."

It's all her fault. Everything that is wrong came from her.

"And when did I ever ask you to do that? When did I ever ask you to pick up after me?" Kira leaned forward. "I'm a grown woman, for fuck's sake. I can make my own decisions."

"I don't believe you can right now. Look at you."

"And that's just it, Mum. You've never ever believed in me. Never. Just for once it would be nice if you gave me some fucking encouragement!"

"Now just a second, young lady. I am trying to have a civil conversa..."

"No you're not. You're trying to control me just like you always have. Chipping away at me, putting me down."

"I'm what!"

"You heard, Mum." Kira was standing now, her hands planted firmly on the table top. "You're never satisfied with anything I do. Nothing is ever good enough. And whenever I need your support it's always on your terms."

It has always been her. You need to get rid of her.

"Kira!" Connie forced the name out like a whip crack.

You'd be better if she was gone. The anguish gone. That cloying inescapable control gone. Freedom. Freedom to do what you want. To live your life for you.

"What!"

"Don't you use that tone on me, young lady." Connie stood tall, her chair thrust back, mirroring her daughter, challenging her. "I've a good mind to..."

"Just shut up, Mum. Shut the fuck up! I've had it with you."

"How dare you speak to me like that!"

You need to do it, Kira. You need to take your chance. You need to live! Do it, Kira. Do it now!

"Shut up!"

The knife was in Kira's hand without her realising. Everything hushed – her mother and the voice inside her head. Time slowed. She could see each individual droplet of rain as it struck then ran down the outside of the kitchen window. The beat of her heart slowed as a feeling of calm reassurance swept through her. Her arm arced wide and far. Her mother's mouth gaped and her eyes widened. A hand came up too slowly to offer any resistance, the fingertips millimetres beneath the sweep of the knife. Metal connected with skin. And then time reset.

A scream. A fine spray. A gurgle.

Then blackness.

~

"The psychiatrist is here now, Ma'am."

Detective Inspector Mitchell raised her head, glad to have a distraction from the paperwork spread across the desk. Every little detail was being committed to memory. Each piece of evidence compartmentalised as she tried to pull together the jigsaw puzzle of the murder. An intelligent young lady with no history of violence or any prior encounters with the law was now sitting in one of their cells with the blood of her mother on her hands. That young lady was almost catatonic – just simple grunts and whimpers when asked questions.

The neighbours had found her sitting in a pool of her mother's blood, a sticky black puddle seeping into her leggings as she stared into the far distance. The cause of death was obvious and there was no doubt she had committed it. But there was no motive as to why. No discernible clue or indication as to what had made her snap. Friends and family had spoken of a close relationship between mother and daughter; how the mother had doted on her, helping her through her illness, giving up everything to give her daughter the life she wanted her to have. They had even been seen hugging on the doorstep the evening that it happened. So the why remained a mystery and the answers were locked inside the young woman's head. And she was hoping this was going to be the key.

"Send him in."

The officer exited the doorway to be replaced by an older, more portly gentleman.

"John, good to see you. Please take a seat."

"Sarah." He nodded in welcome, removing

his coat and putting it on the back of the chair. "How are you? Kids well?"

She laughed a joyless laugh. "They're good, when their father allows me to see them."

"Oh, I'm sorry to hear that." He took a seat, lost for anything further to add.

Sarah sighed. "Shall we get down to business?"

"Of course," he said, a little too eagerly. "What do you have for me today?"

"Matricide, I'm afraid, John. Daughter in her twenties killed her mother for no apparent reason in the family home."

Sarah noted the twinge in John's face as she continued to reel out the details. She saw him peering over his glasses to glance at the photos on the desk as she mentioned the knife and how they found mother and daughter.

"So we need you to help us understand what drove Kira to do this to her mother."

"Kira, did you say?"

"Yes, Kira, um," she looked to her notes, "Kira Jones. Why?"

He picked up one of the pictures from the table; turning it to face him, taking a closer look. The one of Kira, her clothes stained dark.

Recognition flickered, the blood draining from his face, his ruddy visage becoming pale and waxy.

"John, are you okay?"

"I'm, I'm fine. I just need a second." He took three deep breaths, his Adam's apple rising and falling as he composed himself. "I'm sorry, Sarah. I really am sorry but I'm afraid I can't do this."

"For fuck's sake, John. Why not?" She tried to keep the frustration from her voice but lack of sleep wasn't helping. "You've helped on a number of cases before. It's not as if this is new to you."

John Secombe paused to remove his glasses, taking a small cloth from his pocket to wipe them, before replacing them on his nose. He stared forlornly at the picture in his hand, wondering just where he had gone wrong. Where he could have made a better judgement call. The lie about the device was necessary, as was the faked surgery. But there had been no other way. There was nothing anyone else had been able to do for her.

He thought back to their first meeting and everything had been apparent then. Kira's illnesses were psychosomatic, so why couldn't the cure come from within her? Simple hypnotic suggestion reinforced over and over again. And she had shown good signs of progress. Excellent signs in fact. But he had missed something, and he would question what that was well beyond his retirement.

Sitting in a cell a few corridors away, Kira stared at the blank wall opposite her. Police officers had come and gone but she had not noticed them in the same way that the cell, the building, the entire outside world didn't really exist for her. She was here now with her mother, and all Kira could do was apologise time and again for what she had done. Beg forgiveness. Ask for her mother to understand. Wanting to turn back the clock to before she had ever even heard of Pam, or Dr Secombe or nanotechnology. And all her mother said in return was the same simple phrase.

That's a shame, love. That's a shame.

Discomfort
Food

The food mocked her. A self-knowing, irreverent mock.

The burgers had come from work, packed in a brown paper bag with Smithy's Steaks' double S picked out starkly in red. The bottom of the bag was covered with a greasy, dark splotch, leeching meat juices and cooking oils onto the peeling veneer of the coffee table, mingling among the coffee cup rings which formed a haphazard Olympic flag.

The food had been congealing for a good fifteen minutes, sitting idly in the lounge while Rebecca removed her uniform in the bedroom. The limp blue flannel t-shirt had been flung onto her single bed along with the matching cap emblazoned with the double S. The food waited for her, watching through the open door as she eased herself from the rest of her clothes and went to wash off the grime of the day. Ten minutes of hot soapy water showered away the grease of the restaurant, the steam condensing steadily on the flat's mould framed windows.

She had never understood why Smithy's insisted on calling itself a restaurant; there was no rest to be had. Not for the staff nor for the customers. Order, fry, serve and smile, order, fry, serve and smile, ad infinitum; a constant conveyor belt of drudge. Occasionally there would be a customer complaint to spice things up, a moan about the lack of sauce on their burger or the tepidity of their coffee, but an extra portion of fries invariably stopped the caterwauling.

Still, all the drudgery was done for today. The only thing which existed in the here and now was her, the snugness of her bathrobe, and Smithy's Steaks' supersized triple decker cheeseburger with fries and accompanying side of fried onion rings all to be washed down with an extra thick chocolate milkshake.

Each portion was removed from the bag with care, almost reverentially, the food laid out in precise order; a perverse holy trinity. First came the burger wrapped in its wax coated paper, followed by the fries poking from the top of their specially-cut cardboard envelope which, like the burger, had the double S plastered all over the packaging. Finally, the onion rings. Her personal favourite. Three delicious circles of oil-saturated yumminess. An especially thick ring tumbled to the floor, darting for freedom as she lifted the miniature pack from the bag. Driven by instinct, Rebecca plucked it from the floor and dusted it off, ignoring the fluff which drifted away from the crust. The three second rule was a given in her household. Satisfied, she put it back in its pack and straightened the line of food, grabbing her drink once she was content.

The condensation coating the milkshake was cold but not unpleasant. She sucked greedily on the straw; the inside of her cheeks drew inwards, her face resembling a duck's arse, as she drew the first globs of ice-chilled chocolate milk up through the tube – a colonic in reverse.

"We know what you did."

It was the burger who spoke first. It always was. The lips of the bun quivering marginally with each syllable, exposing the cheese-draped meat inside. A sliver of lettuce fell from its mouth as it continued.

"We heard it all from the freezer room."

Rebecca slurped on.

"It's true," interjected the fries, an excited twittering of voices, high pitched like a nest of sparrows tweeting in unison.

"We know you didn't mean to." She watched helplessly as the onion rings joined in, each circle flexing to form a mouth. "Someone was bound to do it at some point, it just happened to be you."

"Don't make excuses for her," snapped the cheeseburger, a spurt of special sauce squirting from its lips in disgust. "She knew full well what she was doing! Didn't you."

"I didn't." The words burbled through a mouthful of chilled ecstasy. "It was an accident."

"See," chimed the rings, "we told you she didn't mean to."

"Well you're a fool then," spat the burger. "I don't know why you are defending her. You know she doesn't think of you in that way."

Rebecca could have sworn there was a wink, a sly crease from the top of the sesame encrusted bun directed at the onion rings.

"Don't know what you mean," they spluttered, a flush of embarrassment spreading rosy red across the batter.

The fries chimed in with a lilting song full of mocking. "The onions love Rebecca, the onions love Rebecca. You want to hug her, you want to..."

They never completed their childish rendition; burgers, fries and rings all caught without warning in the sweep of her arm, scattering across the dark weave of the rose patterned carpet.

They all lay there unmoving, mingling with the vulgarity of the fibres underfoot, a swirling mishmash of purples and reds leftover from the previous tenant.

For the second time that week she collected the dustpan and brush, grabbing it from the recesses of the kitchen. The thin bristles of the brush swept up the silenced food, dragging it from the floor into the pan. The more stubborn pieces were left to her stubby fingers to deal with, picking them from the weave of the carpet.

When she thought she had every last piece she marched them into the kitchen, a bizarre funeral procession of one. Her toes found the pedal for the bin, lifting the lid to dump her accusers – and her admirer, she shivered at the thought – into its guts.

Voices called to her from the darkness of the tomb, last night's dinner hollering at her to be freed along with tonight's captives. Calls of "murderess" and "hussy" rose up from the depths of the cheap aluminium bin, deadened in part by the white polythene liner. Turning, Rebecca walked on, the sound of the closing bin lid echoing behind her within the confines of the kitchen. The shouts continued unabated, but she ignored the protestations and shuffled back to the sofa.

The cushions welcomed her bulk, closing in around her as she slumped back down, easing herself into their embrace. Her arm flopped to the right, grabbing her drink for the comfort of the remaining chocolate milk. It took a moment before the gherkin slice caught her eye, partially camouflaged against green leaves stitched into the carpet among the maroon. She struggled free from the warmth of the cushions, standing up to tread on the offending salad, smushing it into the carpet, feeling the squelch of it as it spread across the sole of her bare foot. She didn't care, she would do anything to stop it staring at her so accusingly.

~

Harsh, electronic tones woke her from darkness. There were no dreams to disturb her anymore, not since last week. No more images of the perverse or the perverted, nothing to make her wake gasping for breath, her bedclothes soaked with sweat. Those were long gone. It was as if her subconscious had decided enough was enough and run away screaming to the hills. And, she thought, who could blame it.

She stretched out an arm, feeling the solid form of the clock under her fist, the buzzing replaced by a thud as it fell to the floor from the bedside table. Red digits glared back from the carpet, meeting her gaze from the side of the bed, her head poking from under the covers.

"Shit!"

She was late. If she was quick it wouldn't matter too much. If.

Throwing the sheets aside, she rushed into the bathroom, grabbing a threadbare towel from the back of the door on her way. Tossing it over the frame, she squeezed herself into the shower cubicle, fingers hunting for the start button. Pipes chuntered. Water flowed. She arched her back against the cascading shower, flinching as she waited for the boiler to kick in and send some warm water through the system.

And then there was heat. A subtle change in temperature. The soft, warm breath of someone standing behind her. Her skin goose-pimpled. Warmth dripped down the inside of her legs, a golden trickle running down her thighs. She watched impotently as straw coloured waters pooled around her feet. There were two shadows in the confines of the cubicle, hers and *his*. After all, who else would it be but *him*, *his* coarse hands grabbing her biceps, *his* fingers digging into her sagging flesh. *His* fingernails were ragged, four of them missing completely from fingers covered in blistered skin. Yellowing bone poked through the flesh in flashes of colour, contrasting with the ripe pink surrounding it, the pus of decay oozing from the open wounds.

Rebecca turned. She didn't want to. She wanted to run screaming from the shower, flee out of the flat and into the street, to get out of there as quickly as possible with the water still clinging to her naked body. But she didn't. All she could do was turn and face *him*, face what she had created. So she looked, taking it all in, feasting on the thing before her. And then everything faded to black.

~

The shower woke her, beating down on her bright red skin, the water warm enough to be uncomfortable but not enough to leave blisters. She wobbled as she stood, dragging herself up from the ground using the shower hose as a crude rope. She stood alone. There was no sign of *him*, or that *he* had ever been there.

The thought to phone in sick crossed her mind, to tell them she was not going to be in today. But then what? Stay at home with nothing to do except think about *him*, or maybe she could go talk to her dinner, see if it had come round to forgiving her yet.

She slunk out of the cubicle and dried herself.

The towel was as effective as a napkin, envelope thin and sopping wet before the job was halfway done. She shrugged herself into her work clothes, the fabric clinging to the parts of her body which refused to dry. Halfway decent, she glanced at the digital numbers as they ticked over. 10:53.

"I might just make it," she thought, the eternal cry of the naïve optimist, except she was neither.

Metal scraped on wood as Rebecca snatched up her keys from the hallway shelf, the pile of mail she'd left unopened tumbling to the floor in her haste. A band of red flashed at her from behind a cellophane window, the word FINAL typed in bold letters. It would have to wait.

Sprinting as best she could, Rebecca took the steps two at a time, rushing down the communal stairwell and out into the street. If she was quick she could get the number 57 to work for 11.15am; still late but not by much.

The number 57 was sailing away into the distance as she lurched up to the bus stop, drawing in great sobs of air as her lungs screamed in pain.

~

"And good morning to you."

The firmly folded arms suggested it was anything but a good morning in Trevor's world. Trevor, or Tre-voor as he pronounced it, like a donkey braying for attention, was the new interim duty manager, rushed in from Smithy's Steaks' head office. He was climbing the managerial chain, only twenty-two years of age and already privileged with the recipe for the secret sauce.

Tre-voor simply stood there, his eyes focused directly on Rebecca, an unwavering stare which demanded respect. Rebecca had to look up to meet his gaze – the alternative was to stare somewhere around his sternum. She chose the latter. She didn't need to look him in the face to know he was raising an eyebrow.

"Well?" The tone enough to suggest his other eyebrow had joined its companion in climbing towards the peak of his perfectly presented cap.

"Oh, um, good morning," she mumbled towards his chest, making to walk round him, an overwhelming urge to dump her jacket in the staff room.

"That's it?

"Good morning...sir?"

Jumped up little prick, she thought, hoping the last bit hadn't been spoken out loud.

"Better, but I would also like to know," he raised his bare right arm, rotating it in what looked like the start of an audacious salute before bringing his wrist level with his eyes. Rebecca snorted a laugh, unable to help herself. "I would also," he continued, ignoring the outburst, "like to know, why you think it acceptable to be forty seven minutes late for your shift."

"Women's problems."

He looked puzzled, as if his staff member were speaking a different language.

"You know," she dropped her voice, "down there." He followed the direction of her extended finger, his face flushing red as his eyes met the zipper of her work issued trousers.

His face didn't know what to do, his eyes searching out the corners of the room, skirting the floor tiles, examining the lights, flitting anywhere except Rebecca.

"Is that all?" she asked.

"Um, yes, that's all."

She muttered *Prick* under her breath as she brushed past him.

~

"What happened to you?" asked Cathy, leaning against the kitchen worktop, filing her nails as she spoke.

"Overslept," Rebecca lied, portioning out paper cups into small, medium, large and super-size. Cathy was the closest thing Rebecca had to a friend at work, they had both started at the same time last year, but she wasn't about to tell Cathy the real reason she hadn't made it in on time.

"Did the new guy read you the riot act?" Cathy didn't wait for a reply, taking it as read Rebecca wouldn't have got off lightly. "He's a bit of a dick but at least he's not as creepy as Rupert was. Give him a manager's badge and suddenly old Roops thinks he has open access to everything about you."

Rebecca continued stacking cups, used to Cathy's diatribes. She often suspected Cathy would be an amazing singer, someone who didn't seem to need to pause for breath no matter how long they spoke for.

"One day," Cathy dropped her voice to a whisper, "I caught him peering into the ladies' changing room, fucking pervert. Well, I gave him what for, I can tell you. I'll bet that's the last time he tried that with anyone else."

Rebecca moved on to napkins, tearing open the polythene wrapper and stacking them into the square metal containers. Smithy's liked to give the air of an American diner – the fact the first restaurant had opened in Dudley didn't matter one jot.

"I reckon head office caught wind of it, you know. Someone grassed him up. I bet it was Cheryl. He always had a thing for Cheryl. They whipped him out and shifted in robot boy with all his 'subsection this and paragraph that' of the rule book. I'd put money on it."

"Do you think we could change the subject?" snapped Rebecca.

"Oooh, get you." Cathy put down her nail file. "Sounds like you would have been better staying in bed. It's okay, I'm meant to be out on counter anyways."

"Sorry, I just don't want to talk management. Friends?"

"Sure, hon, don't sweat it. And, sweetie, get some sleep. You look like crap. In a nice way."

She blew a kiss in Rebecca's direction as she left. Few people could get away with talking to Rebecca like that but Cathy was definitely one of them.

Rebecca sighed to herself, looking at the remaining stack of napkins. Once those were done, she needed to refill the paper bags for the drive-thru. She got all the good jobs. At least she wasn't on the counter. She didn't think she could deal with serving food today, each portion potentially screaming her guilt. It took her a moment to notice the sound behind her.

Footsteps. Wet, limping footsteps. She didn't dare turn. Her neck prickled with heat, breath pluming against her skin.

"Rebecca," her name whispered on the breeze, three syllables mingling with the strands of her hair. "Rebecca." This time the word was purred as fingers caressed the nape of her neck, drifting round to cradle her throat. The aroma of roasted pork filled the air, a sweet, meaty goodness overpowering the grease tinged stench, yet it was wrong, oh so wrong. If she turned around she would be able to taste it, embrace it, and hold it forever. Her neck craned slowly...

"Rebecca," shouted Greg, one of her fellow wage slaves, as he ghosted round the corner, "The boss wants you."

~

The door was awkward as Rebecca pushed against it, catching on the fraying carpet. It was the first time she had been allowed in the manager's office. No one had ever been allowed inside when Rupert was in charge. The staff joked it was where he used to go to jerk off over his girlie magazines...or they did when he was still there.

There was little of any note: a filing cabinet to the left with a pile of staff manuals stacked on top. To the right was the safe where all the takings for the day were stored. Beside the safe rested the ubiquitous fire extinguisher which graced every room in Smithy's restaurant; health and safety in all things.

On the rear wall was a picture of old Donovan Smith, founder and owner of Smithy's Steaks, standing proudly in front of his first store, his gut pressing against the buttons of his suit jacket whilst his balding head reflected the beaming sun. He gazed down on the managerial desk which dominated the room, a huge piece of cheap pine covered with paperwork, monitors, and the hunched figure of Tre-voor tapping away at his laptop. One of Smithy's specials lay untouched beside him, a triple chilli burger with accompanying fries and shake.

"You wanted to see me?"

Tre-voor looked up from his work, his chair squeaking as he swivelled around. There was something different about him, an air of increased confidence, less concerned about the social intricacies which came with discussions of the menstrual cycle.

"It would have been polite to knock." He waved away her protestations with a flick of his hand. "Come here. I want you to take a look at this."

Her natural inclination was to slap some manners across his face, but something told her now was neither the time nor place.

"Better," he said, watching as she shuffled forward. "Now..." His phone rang, the *Star Wars* theme blaring from his pocket. He silenced it and continued. "Now, I think you have some explaining to do."

On the screen of his laptop was a still image of the kitchen area, grainy and monochrome, flickering slightly as the screen fought to hold the resolution. Rebecca took another step forward. In the image were two ghosts, pictures from history. The first was Rupert, tall and gangly, a Tre-voor clone if ever there was one. There was probably a factory where they churned out duty managers, cardboard cut-outs ready to bark orders at junior staff. The second was Rebecca.

The cursor flicked across the screen, resting on the pause button, changing it to play. The image juddered into life, replaying a nightmare Rebecca had already lived through.

The date stamp was from the previous week, seconds ticking past in the bottom right hand corner of the image as the restaurant shut down for the night. Rupert had asked her to stay late with a promise of double wages. Just the two of them with everyone else clocked off for the night.

Rebecca wanted to shout the words which went with the silent images. To narrate the bit where the camera angle hid Rupert's sticky hands as they pawed at her breasts, his breath hot on her neck, to scream the part where she told him to stop it or else, the bit where he backed out of shot and pulled his small, thin cock out and started stroking it, asking if she wanted a go. The camera missed where he called her a frigid, fat bitch and said that he was going to fire her if she didn't get down on all fours and come suck him off there and then.

It missed all those bits. It did capture the glint of metal when the knife found its way into her hand. It did capture the spurts of blood showing black across her pale face. And it did show the sanity-loosened smile creeping across her lips.

Tre-voor stopped it there. Rebecca imagined he did it for decency. She imagined he did it because he didn't have the stomach to watch the gruelling hour she spent slicing the flesh from Rupert's bones, feeding it into the deep fat fryer, then putting the cooked meat into the waste product bags ready for collection the next day. She imagined he didn't want to watch as she took a meat tenderiser and smashed his bones into shards and dust, flushing what she could down the toilets before realising it would be easier to drop them straight down the industrial sized drains outside. She wondered if he had watched fascinated as the leftover food on the counters started taunting her, telling her she was going to get caught, that she should have simply done as he asked and then cried herself to sleep every night for the rest of her life.

"I have to inform you that I have let HR know about this."

Oh my God, the prick didn't even call the police.

She imagined him pawing through the employee manual, finding a page which said any incident must be reported to head office in the first instance and then waiting for further instruction. *Dick!*

'*Told you, you would get caught,*' the chilli burger on his desk piped up.

"Shut up," she hissed.

"I most certainly will not shut up." Trev-oor raised himself higher in his chair as he spoke, adjusting the specially branded tie which only managers were allowed to wear.

'*You should have just done what he wanted and be done with it.*'

"Shut your filthy mouth."

"I beg your pardon. Do you know who you are speaking to!"

'*You're going to spend the rest of your life in jail where they'll pass you round like the cheap piece of meat that you are.*"

"I said shut up!"

The sound of the fire extinguisher connecting with his skull was an unusual noise, a dull clang, much as she imagined swinging a wet pillow into a church bell might sound. There were no cartoon tweety birds circling his head, forming an unholy halo of chirping cheeriness. Just the dull echo of metal mashing into flesh, compacting into bone, flecks of red paint mingling with the deep, treacly crimson oozing from his cracked skull.

The papers on Tre-voor's desk bowed under the weight of the extinguisher as she set it to one side. A pool of blood was collecting on the laminated surface, seeping into the stack of last month's sales.

Head office won't be pleased. The thought caught her unawares, stretching her mouth into a smile, her chest rising and falling as she fought to supress the giggling madness within her. And then it was out, a high pitched, incessant laughter, bouncing round the confines of the tiny office, echoing back at her only to be amplified by a chorus of foodstuffs joining her in the joke.

Except the burger. It was always the burger which brought things back to reality.

'Head office won't be pleased about this one little bit,' it said, struggling to be heard above the cacophony of hyenas in the room. Except she did hear it, she heard every single word and her world came crashing down.

An icon was flashing on the laptop, a smiling anthropomorphic envelope pulsing, waiting for her attention. *'See me! Watch me! Open me!'* it demanded, persistently throbbing like an epileptic's worst nightmare.

And so she clicked it.

Re: You need to see this

It was from head office. She couldn't tell which department. Maybe it was just a picture of some funny cats, some cute, wonderful, adorable cats. That's what the internet was for, surely. Spreading feline joy.

She knew it had nothing to do with cats.

She double clicked the header.

Trevor,

Thank you for your email. We have reviewed the video.

Do nothing. We have phoned the police and they will be there soon. Whatever you do, do not engage the employee in any discussion around the issue.

We have tried calling you with no success. We will continue to do so.

Regards

HR

If she hadn't been at the centre of this shit storm she would have found the email amusing in its formality, imagining some faceless corporate drone sitting at head office formalising wording which should simply have said, 'Get out of there! That lady, she crazy!'

Tre-voor buzzed. Or more precisely, his trouser pocket did so, *Star Wars* echoing once more from his nether regions.

"That will be head office."

Rebecca glanced in the direction of the know-it-all burger, spouting its unasked-for observations. If anything, it looked smug, an expression of 'I told you so' plastered across its seeded bready brow.

"Fuck you!"

The 'you' was punctuated with the impact of the fire extinguisher driven with as much force as she could muster into the obnoxious little shit. Special sauce splayed out across the desk, spattering the parts of Tre-voor's face which were not covered with blood, making him look like a Jackson Pollock masterpiece.

She heard a gasp from the fries but they didn't dare say anything, knowing they could easily be next in line. Maybe it was the skewed smile on her face which silenced them, the glint of uncertainty in her eye. Maybe. Part of her wanted them to speak out, to challenge her sanity and ask what the hell was she doing but she didn't think she had the answer to the question. So she turned her back and left, letting the extinguisher drop limply from her hand, hitting the carpeted floor with a dull thud. The door shut behind her with John Williams still playing in the background.

~

The corridor was empty beyond Tre-voor's office, the strip lighting and lack of windows making it impossible to tell what time of day it was. To her left lay the exit and to the right the kitchen area. She did the only sensible thing she could and turned left.

Maybe it was instinct, maybe it was blind luck, but something made her look up at the security monitor by the exit. There were two men and a woman outside, all in uniform, conferring with each other. Another five seconds and she would have walked straight into their waiting arms. Retracing her steps, she ghosted past the muffled sounds of Tre-voor's phone, ignoring it, moving head down into the kitchen area.

The place was a hive of activity, members of staff flipping burgers, dunking fries and portioning out pre-chopped tomatoes, onions and pickles. She pulled her cap down over her face, trying to hide herself from the attention of her colleagues, making a beeline for the customer counter beyond the shelves of readymade burgers and the freedom of the open restaurant. She froze.

Through the gaps in the shelving she could make out the blue and white uniform of a police officer talking in hushed tones with Cathy. By the time Cathy turned to point in her direction, Rebecca was gone, moving to the back of the kitchen, out to the storeroom, to be anywhere but there.

The hard wood of the door took the weight of her back as she slumped against it. Rows and rows of produce stood stacked across the shelving: burger buns, crates of lettuce and tomatoes, drums of frying oil next to ten kilogram bags of pre-cut French fries ready for cooking.

Voices chirped in unison, squeaks muffled by

cellophane wrapping. It was hard to make out the words initially, the sound more like the chirruping of crickets, slowly building into a dawn chorus.

"In here! She's in here. Murderess! Murderess! Come get her!"

"Shut up!" she hissed. "Shut up, shut up, shut up!"

They ignored her, shouting, pressing against the plastic which held them. Buns and fries started falling from the shelves, overbalancing in their eagerness.

From the other side of the door she could hear shouting.

"Anyone seen Rebecca?"

"Does anyone know where she is?"

And then a scream. The kind of scream which meant someone would never, ever be able to sleep with the lights off again. The sort of scream that happens when someone has found a skull half caved in by a blunt object.

Rebecca ran to the far end of the room, bags of buns popping as her bulk squeezed the air out of them. Her footing gave, slipping on the slime of overripe tomatoes, her fall cushioned by the taunting buns.

The solid steel door at the end of the room dominated her view as she looked up. She could hide in there. Things would be quiet inside. No one would think her crazy enough to do that.

She could feel French fries crawling up her ankles, trying to prevent her from getting up, but she shrugged them off with a flick of her heel.

Beyond the door there were footsteps, people running to the scream, scared and curious, the morbid fascination with the unknown. And still no one had tried the storeroom.

The rubber coated handle to the freezer opened easily, the digital display above it reading minus twenty degrees. There would be no one to criticise her inside, each piece of meat was frozen solid, in deep stasis until needed. She didn't think the food in the storeroom would give her away, not if she was out of sight. She stepped inside, clouds of white flowing in front of her face.

The door was stubborn to close but she managed it with effort, a dull click bringing darkness with it. She was right, there was no chattering in here, no one to chastise her. With hands thrust out and knees bent, she found her way to the back of the room, using the stacked boxes of frozen burgers for guidance.

Shivering, she slid herself to the floor, the cold seeping through her clothes. It was fine. It would all be fine. She could sit here until it was all over. Wait for the commotion to die down. She would be able to explain everything then, tell everyone it wasn't her fault. For now she could sleep. Rest a while. Close her eyes.

Except she wouldn't be able to do any of those things. She knew he wouldn't let her. Each puff of breath on the back of her neck told her so.

The Man Who Fed the Foxes

Paul Wilson sat alert on the decking, peering into the gloom. Even if the sun had been high in the sky rather than cresting the horizon, as it currently was, there wouldn't be much to see. An overgrown garden in need of an industrial lawnmower and a team of willing volunteers. At the end stood a broken greenhouse, barely five years old yet virtually forgotten, the glass fractured and smeared the colour of pond scum by a colony of algae. A couple of abandoned compost bins nestled beside it, like giant salt and pepper shakers, overflowing and surrounded by flowering weeds. His borders, which had been so immaculate in a former life, flourishing with begonias, tulips and carefully cultivated roses, were now clogged with bindweed, nettles and dandelions. His lawn had once been his pride and joy, manicured to the millimetre, but that was in the past when his friends used to joke you could have played crown green bowls on it. Not that his friends visited any more.

Paul was a reflection of his garden; shabby, unkempt, in need of attention. A scarecrow man, broken and forgotten. His shirt, stained with last night's dinner, was fraying at the seams, struggling to contain his middle aged spread, his jeans more holes than fabric, the denim pale and faded. His hair used to be a uniform short back and sides but now hung lankly in a mix of browns and greys against his shoulders, blending with the beard that was home to the yellowed, crusted yolk from that morning's fried egg sandwich.

Not that any of it mattered much in the great scheme of things. If nature wanted to claim his garden then let her, it had been hers to begin with anyway. And as for his friends, well, if they didn't want him then he certainly didn't want them and that suited him fine. Just fine. He had other things to occupy his time.

Paul dragged his blanket closer, warding off the chill as the summer air cooled around him, the tartan pattern ruffling as he struggled to get comfortable. Cheap plastic creaked and cracked in protest, the chair complaining beneath his weight, but it held, ready to see out another night.

On the lawn, less than ten feet away, a haze of flies were squabbling around the meat. They did so most nights. He always placed it there, never nearer, never further, carefully positioned so as to be far enough from the decking but close enough to give him a clear view. The cloud of insects performed a little dance; fly, land, suck and twirl; fly, land, suck and twirl; repeated like a miniature troop of Morris men performing for the crowds. Except there was only Paul who watched on, struggling to keep track of their flights in the worsening light. The offering wasn't for them but it didn't matter. There was plenty more meat to be had.

Next to the meat was a bowl of milk, curdled in the heat of the day, a viscous skin crusting its surface. The letters D O G were embossed on the brown glazed ceramic, though it had been years since they had owned any pets. The bowl had belonged to Shandy, a canine substitute for the children they never had, not that they would have ever admitted such a thing to themselves. Shandy had been gone for nearly a decade – they never said dead, always gone – and Paul couldn't bring himself to get a replacement. It seemed such a callous act of betrayal. *She* had asked Paul a hundred times to throw the bowl out and threatened on more than one occasion to do it herself. *She* had said that about a lot of things but he always ignored her, always loathe to throw anything away, a hoarder then and a hoarder still, but the one thing he hadn't been able to keep hold of was her.

So now he sat here alone of an evening, every evening, watching and waiting for the foxes to come. But none came that night.

The last 'friend' to visit was Rachel Gladstone, all full of concern and nosiness. That had been six months ago, long before the foxes.

Ding dong.

He jumped, it had been so long since anyone had rung his doorbell. Paul waited. Whoever it was might go away. He was comfortably cocooned in his living room, nursing a glass of cheap rioja, soothing the world away. He had sat in the exact same way for several weeks now, huddled into his armchair for hours on end. There was routine to his life, a routine he liked. Get up, wash (optional), throw on some clothes and face the trials and tribulations of the day all delivered through his television set. Now and again he might be so bold as to attempt a jigsaw. Something classic depicting battles from the Napoleonic era, officers in blood stained uniforms barking out orders whilst grand explosions ballooned in the background. He enjoyed the banality of it all. The simplicity. There were no grey areas, no ambiguity. Either the piece fitted or it did not. And when the last piece was down he could settle back with his wine for company.

Ding dong.

Sit and wait them out. There was his answer. No one could be that concerned about him. Probably one of those Jehovah's come to spread the good word. There had been enough good words from friends in the past months; not one of them changed anything, not one of them stopped the tears from soaking his pillow every night. He took another sip of wine, enjoying the numbing feeling creeping across his forehead.

Out of the corner of his eye he saw something twitch. A silhouette at the window.

Bugger. He should have hidden. Perhaps slunk behind the sofa out of sight. Maybe they hadn't seen him. It was dark in here and they could mistake him for a pile of dirty laundry abandoned for later.

Tap, tap, tap.

The sound of knuckles rapping against his windowpanes. And waving. There was waving now, definitely in his direction.

"Paul, Paul, yoo-hoo, it's Rachel." The words were muffled as they came through the glass, like someone shouting through a towel.

He inwardly shuddered. Rachel. Rachel Gladstone. Rachel bloody Gladstone.

A local snoop with nothing better in her life than to live through the lives of others. She reminded him of a parasite, a bloated leech which kept sucking and sucking until it eventually fell off. But she never did. This was the third time she had visited since Amelia had gone. He knew from past experience he would have to let her in. The tenacious bloody leech.

"My God, you look terrible." Those were the first words from her mouth as he opened the door.

Rachel bloody Gladstone. As delicate as ever. He was inclined to slam the door in her puffy little face right there and then but he knew it would cause more aggravation in the long run. Get more people poking their nose in where it wasn't wanted. He smiled sweetly and stood aside.

"How lovely to see you, Rachel," (lie), "Won't you come in?"

She didn't wait for a second invitation, shoving her way past him, her sensible shoes trailing mud across the threshold from the soil beneath his front window. In her hand was a hessian bag, the word *Waitrose* emblazoned on the side to show the world what a good person she was, one who thought about the environment by not needlessly wasting plastic carriers. It sagged in the middle like its owner.

"Now, I hope you don't mind, but I've brought you some...oh."

Paul knew what had stopped her mid-sentence, he could smell the snobbery wafting off her in waves. He could hear the sound of the cogs whirring in her elitist skull full of its airs and graces, judging the disarray which was his house. He shut the door and followed her into the living room.

"Some what, Rachel?" He kept his tone flat, not caring what she had brought with her. He wanted her in and out, and anything which sped that up was fine by him.

"Some, um..." She stepped over a pair of discarded pizza boxes and shuffled towards the armchair. That had been Amelia's chair when she lived here. It wasn't anymore. Now it housed a mountain of circulars, fallen through the letterbox and dumped there unopened, a nest of false promises to improve one's life. One day Paul would get around to throwing them away. One day.

"Some...?" ventured Paul. He picked up his abandoned wine glass and filled it, disinclined to offer Rachel any.

"Some dinner." She dipped into her bag, flourishing a Tupperware container filled with something which resembled a casserole or stew. Her gaze fell back to the pizza boxes. "Though I see you seem to be looking after yourself..." she sucked at her teeth, searching for the right word, "...admirably."

That wrinkle of the nose as she finished her sentence. He had forgotten about the wrinkle. God, how he hated the wrinkle. Paul sipped his wine, draining a third of the glass before it left his lips.

"Thank you, very kind. If you could leave it on the side."

"Paul?"

Oh God, she's perching. She's actually bloody perching.

The Tupperware disappeared back into the bag as she cleared a space on the arm of the sofa, sending an avalanche of junk mail crashing to the floor. She ignored this and carried on; after all, it wasn't as if she was making the place anymore untidy then it already was.

Paul took another swig of his wine and topped up his glass.

"Paul, I'm worried about you. You haven't been the same since, um, you know, since Amelia."

How would you bloody well know what I was like in the first place? Stupid woman.

He simply stared.

"And, well, I said to myself, Rachel I said, you need to go round there and let that poor man know he's not alone. Show him he has someone to talk to."

Someone to leech off him, you mean.

Another sip. Just a small one.

"So, Paul, how long has it been since, since...Amelia and him?"

There it was. There was the rub. This was the blood money she wanted for her homemade casserole. To hear about *him*. *Her*. *Them*.

"I'd rather not talk about it."

Him had been his one-time best friend, or so he had thought at the time. Rhys Davis. God, he wished to this day he had never set eyes on him. Paul had met Rhys at The Griffin's pub quiz. Rhys, new to the area, had sauntered over, asking if he could join Paul and Amelia at their table.

"Room for one more?" was how he had phrased it with his oh-so-easy-going Welsh tones.

Paul hadn't been keen but Amelia had insisted. To Paul's surprise they had hit it off, especially when Rhys got the round in, and before long Rhys became a regular feature round their house, popping round to help with the DIY, and Paul would return the favour, helping Rhys with his garden.

Amelia had welcomed the new friendship, saying it was good to see Paul smiling again.

Things were good. Amelia was more 'friendly' than she had been in years, she had even stopped nagging him about his 'ways' as she called them, the hoarding and the clutter; unfinished puzzles covering any vacant surface in the house. Things were good indeed.

Paul had come home early one evening. He had been at the garden centre for more fertiliser to feed the tomatoes in the greenhouse. Last year's batch had been a poor show and he was determined to give the current crop a fighting chance. He had caught Rhys and Amelia *en flagrante*; that was the term the foreigners used, wasn't it. His best friend and his wife of thirty years playing 'hide the proverbial sausage' in their marital bed.

There had been words, plenty of words, though he couldn't remember many of them. He had blacked out from the stress. He had always been bad at confrontations. Even as a child he would shy away from arguments, quick to anger and quick to flee, running away to hide in the corner until the red mist cleared and the bad words faded into the ether. When he came to with dried tear tracks across his cheeks, there was no sign of the pair of them and Amelia's clothes were gone. For the first few days he stayed at home, waiting patiently for Amelia to tell him she had made a mistake, for her to settle her slight frame down on the sofa and beg for his forgiveness (and he knew he would give it). He busied himself with the garden, potting on his tomatoes, keeping the lawn trim, even tidying away the clutter ready for her return. But she never came back. He tried phoning her mobile with no success. Always to voicemail. Then one day he received a text out of the blue saying to forget about her and that was that. Nothing more.

As word spread across the neighbourhood, he realised he had been the last to know about the affair. Those friends of his who dared to show their faces all used phrases like 'I half suspected as much,' or 'it was inevitable in the end, really.' So he hid away like he had in his childhood. Giving up on his garden and his friends. And no one came to visit him anymore, which he liked. Until today.

"I think you should, Paul. I think you should talk about it. It will be helpful, don't you think?"

"No. No I don't think it would." He surprised himself by speaking out loud. If Rachel heard the anger in his words she ignored it.

"Paul," she murmured, that tone of mock concern stretched over two syllables. The sofa arm creaked as she rose, reaching over to put her arm on his wrist, the touch of a leech sensing sustenance. "Paul, sit down and let's talk about things."

He flinched, flinging her arm away from him, sending an arc of Rioja flying across the room. Deep red seeped into the carpet, flourishing like the bastard child of Rorschach's nightmares. Its twin was spawning over Rachel's outfit, blossoming in her pastel ensemble.

"Now look what you've made me do," he mumbled, turning from her anger. He grabbed for the bottle, desperate to refill his glass and find some small grain of solace from what was left of his afternoon. If he didn't look at her perhaps she would leave.

She didn't.

"What the hell do you think you're doing!" There it was. The veneer dropped, no more sympathy and concern; the monster revealed. He imagined Rachel's face twisting in rage as she spouted behind him, the eyes scrunching into wrinkle encircled raisins, exaggerating her crow's feet. He could hear her lipstick fracture as her lips thinned, the sound of a crème brûleé's crust cracking. He could imagine flakes of red Estee Lauder Pure Colour falling on to her collar, mixed with spittle and rage.

The bottle felt comforting, the familiar feel of the thin neck in his hand, grabbed perhaps a little more tightly than normal. His glass, where was his glass? Dropped when she had touched him. Look for the glass, not at her, keep your eyes on the floor, away from the leech. Oh for some salt!

"I said, what the hell do you think you're doing!"

A hand on his shoulder. Oh God, why did she have to put a hand on his shoulder? Surely she knew he didn't want to be touched. Wasn't that clear? He tensed up. His muscles tightened. His jaw pulsing as his teeth gritted. He gripped the bottle a little tighter still, his knuckles whitening as he spun to face the seething harridan.

Her face was as he imagined, all bile and hate, yet still the countenance of a victim; as if it wasn't her who had come to his house unbidden, nosing into his business. He knew there were going to be more words. Words he didn't want to hear. He would do anything not to hear those words. He shifted his weight, readying himself for the onslaught.

And that was when the blackness took him.

When he came to, he was alone, face down like a murder victim in the centre of his wine stained carpet, the empty bottle lying by his side.

~

No one visited him again. Or no one human. He had become *persona non grata* which suited him fine.

He couldn't remember exactly when the foxes started visiting, or when he started to feed them for that matter. He was no stranger to the foxes, or their nocturnal sounds to be more precise, listening to their lust filled exertions, screeching like fire branded owls as they rutted into the small hours of the night. From time to time he would see a snout poking from the tangle of weeds, sniffing the air, slinking away as soon as they caught his scent. It was like that for months, an occasional sighting followed by a flash of orange and white before the tail disappeared from view. The last thing he expected was for one to brazenly present itself to him.

It had been another night spent in the embrace of his good friend Jack Daniels, waiting for the booze to drag him off to Never Neverland, or whatever place would have him; he was far too old to be a Lost Boy anymore. Caught halfway between sleep and consciousness, he half fancied he saw a flickering of activity in the long grass around his compost bins. Not that they had seen any use in the days since *then*. It had been his plan to make his own compost to feed his soon-to-be prize winning tomatoes; trips to buy fertiliser only carried bitter memories for him. But the plan never grew much beyond conception, leaving the bins to stand as further testament to his failures in life as his tomatoes withered and died.

The movement flickered again, more definite this time, a parting of the grasses and nettles between the bins. It was the snout he saw first, a red furred cone sporting a shock of white on the underside and tipped with a shiny black button. His initial inclination had been to throw his empty bottle of Jack in its general direction. On a rarer, soberer night he might have made the effort. Maybe. But tonight the familiar 'buzz' had claimed him, easing him into the role of witness rather than participant.

Eyes, ears and a neck came next followed by a mangy body, the fur matted in patches against the thin frame, blackened in spots with faeces. Two more heads emerged from either side, squeezing into the space between the composters; Cerberus reborn.

Paul watched impotently as the trio stalked forth, leaving a trail of flattened grass in their wake. They paused momentarily amongst the sprawl of grasses, sniffing at a handful of pizza crusts he had thrown out for the birds into the centre of his lawn.

Scavengers, thought Paul, sighing internally *blooming scavengers. At least you're more honest than some. Well, come take what you want, you're welcome to whatever you can find.*

They ignored the off-casts, slinking onwards towards Paul. And then they stopped, dropping their rears and sitting upright. Three narrow heads staring back at him from barely six feet away.

For a while that was all they did. Sitting and

staring, man and foxes, waiting as the moon rose higher. And then the world changed for Paul forever.

"We know what happened." It was the middle fox who spoke first, the mange-ridden cur, not that the other two looked any healthier.

Paul stared at them, mouth open, waiting for his brain to catch up with the scene. Surely someone would remind him of his lines any time now. The bottle of Jack dropped from his hand, shattering against the floor, a sticky sea of molasses weeping across the patio, bleeding into the cracks, but he didn't care. There was only one thing in his world right now.

"We want to help. We can bring her back," said the one on the left.

"Who?" The word was stuttered, almost scared to be spoken in case the illusion were flung aside to reveal the Great Oz behind the curtain.

"Your bitch. The one you lost." The right one now.

"You, you can't. S-s-she left me...she's gone."

"We know." Mangy turned to its brethren. Paul couldn't tell if it was for reassurance or validation. "We will bring her back."

"She's gone," Paul repeated, his voice close to cracking as he fought the madness seeping into his mind, trying to cling to the one thing he knew for certain. "She's, she's gone."

"We will bring her back," they said as a trio, yipping in unison.

And with that they were gone, turning with a flourish, leaving Paul to watch them weave their way beyond the greenhouse and out into the bushes framing the end of his garden. A final flash of white fur and then they were out of sight.

Clouds trailed lazily across the face of the moon as Paul tried to reconcile what had happened. It was the booze, it had to be the booze. Or a mental breakdown. He had been told it was possible after the experience he had been through. Those were the most plausible explanations. A good night's sleep and things would be clearer in the morning. Hell, he might be asleep now. He pinched two ragged fingernails into his forearm.

"Shit," said Paul to no one in particular, shaking the pain out of his arm, looking at the white crescents forming there. "Not asleep then."

The chair groaned under his weight as he pushed himself out, ready to begin the trudge up to bed. He would clean up the broken bottle in the morning and get a 'fresh' one from his supply under the stairs. It was only as he was rising he noticed the gleam in the grass.

Paul lurched from his chair, a mixture of alcohol and tiredness, shambling his underwhelming physique across the patio as his blanket fell away. He let his legs guide him, only to fall down into the grass where the foxes had spoken. This was where he had seen it. A small rectangular trinket lying amongst the flattened stems, no bigger than a man's palm, catching the broken beams of the full moon. Kneeling, he reached out, his hand trembling as his fingers curled around Amelia's phone.

~

The foxes became regular, though unpredictable, visitors over the following months. One week they would come every day, other times Paul would sit outside, waiting for them, come rain or shine, only to be disappointed when they failed to appear. He was fairly sure they had built themselves an earth at the back of his garden, beyond the slanting shadow of the greenhouse. It was tempting to go exploring, to have a poke around in amongst the weeds to find their bolt hole, except they had an unspoken agreement. A gentleman fox's agreement as it were. The patio and the house behind it were his, the garden theirs. He provided them with food, good food, not scraps, and they provided Amelia.

When not waiting on the patio, he would occupy himself inside. He had a new hobby. A twist on an old favourite. He was building a jigsaw. A life-sized one in his living room. A two hundred and six piece construction. This one didn't come in a box, or not one he was aware of. And the only picture he had to go from was stashed in the attic with his wedding photos.

So the foxes brought Paul his pieces. Sometimes the pieces were large, other times they were of such a size that Paul had to feel his way amongst the grass with his fingertips to find their offering.

If, in his more sober hours, he had broken his gentleman's agreement he would have found the box, or rather boxes, the pieces came in; two flat topped pyramids at the end of his garden which some might say resembled salt and pepper shakers, bought to provide food for his precious tomatoes. But he didn't, and he flourished in his ignorance.

And if his neighbours were ever so inclined as to glance across in the dead of the night they might see a blanketed man crawling on all fours across his lawn. The Rachel Gladstones of this world might have seen such a man disappear into the darkness where the nettles and dandelions clustered around the greenhouse and the composters. None the wiser, they would see him crawl back to his chair, pausing to hide something in the grass, nibbling at the raw meat he had left out which you couldn't find in any butchers local or otherwise, before slumping into his chair and passing out. The Rachel Gladstones of the world would have seen all that if Rachel Gladstone was anywhere to be found.

As it was, Paul Wilson sat night after night, feeding the foxes as they brought his Amelia back home to him.

There Was
an Old Man

"Hurluck! Hurluck!"

John Hinklow was choking. A hacking, vigorous, enthusiastic effort to clear his throat. The kind of exertion a sixty a day smoker would be proud of.

The fly had hit the back of his throat before he realised what was happening, slamming right into the spot where his tonsils used to dangle. Too little too late, the gag reflex had kicked in.

"Hurluck! Hurluck!"

His fingers massaged the wattled flesh of his neck, anything to force the bloody thing from his throat, but it was all in vain. Despite the phantom sensation still hovering in his oesophagus, he knew that it had gaily made its way past his gullet and was readily setting up residence in his stomach. Festering there in his semi-digested breakfast.

It had been buzzing around innocuously, flitting about his head, a minor irritant as he had walked to collect his paper. The paper was part of his ritual. The same ritual every day ever since he had retired ten years ago. Rise at half seven followed by thirty minutes of gentle calisthenics, a brisk cold shower and a shave, then a swift breakfast: probiotic yoghurt, a single boiled egg, a slice of wholemeal toast – dry, naturally – and a dose of multivitamins, all washed down with a freshly squeezed orange juice. After that, come rain or shine, he would venture to Wilkins' for *The Times*, walking the short distance from his house to the newsagents. That was his routine every morning. Had been for the past decade. He liked it. It suited him. It kept him healthy. Everything as it should be. No surprises. That was until today and that wretched, bloody fly.

"Hurluck! Hurluck!"

It was no use. He would just have to accept it. It wasn't going away.

It was the warmth of the day that had attracted it. For months he had been moaning about the bloody cold, seasons not being what they should, poxy hailstorms in June for crying out loud. He'd forgotten that the summer, when it came, brought the pests with it. The plague carriers. Little, flying specks of infestation. They had taught him that at school all those decades ago and he'd lapped it up. Know thy enemy. And he knew them well enough. Shit eaters, that's what they were. They would sit on piles of defecation, sucking it all in only to regurgitate it, eager for a second course. Filthy, disease carrying, airborne vermin. Now one of the little bastards was wallowing in his digestive fluids spreading its pestilence within him. It made him nauseous just thinking about it.

~

The rest of the day had been uneventful. He had collected the paper from Wilkins'. The summer boy had been there, that snotty nosed little oik who clearly had never been introduced to a bar of soap in his life. Fortunately he hadn't had to make physical contact. He was able to retrieve his paper from the pile and swiftly deposit his money on the counter. He always had the correct change, it was a point of principal. No need to take anything from the lad's grubby hands, just drop it down and leave.

Once home, he'd eased himself into his favourite chair overlooking his garden, the lawn well-tended as always, and settled down to read the latest worldly highlights. The usual stuff was there; wars, politics, business, even what passed as celebrity nowadays was making its way into his broadsheet, but he paid little of it any attention today. Today he couldn't get the thought of that fly out of his mind. It was irrational. He knew it was. After all, people swallowed bugs, insects and all other manner of creepy crawlies every day. Wasn't there some damned fool statistic out there about people ingesting eight spiders a year whilst they slept? How the hell does anyone prove that kind of thing? Yet still, he couldn't shake the feeling that it was crawling around inside him, polluting his guts with whatever virulent diseases it was carrying. Oh God, what if it was some sort of foreign super-fly? There'd been a documentary on them, he was sure of it, resistant to the usual pesticides and the like. What if he had one of those in him, what then?

~

"Mr Hinklow, I assure you that you are absolutely fine. For a man of your age you are in near perfect health. Hell, I have patients half your age who would love to be in your condition."

He looked blankly at the doctor sitting there in her comfy chair with her certificates on the wall. He shouldn't have come here. He was beginning to realise it was a stupid mistake. He hated coming to these places. They were filled with sick people. He didn't like sick people. Sick people carried diseases, no better than walking shit eaters themselves.

"And what do you mean by 'my condition'?" he ventured.

"Nothing, Mr Hinklow, it's just a turn of phrase. You have nothing to worry about. You'll more than likely outlive the rest of us if you keep looking after yourself as you do. Now, please, go home, relax and don't give this a second thought."

Relax? How could he go home and relax? There was a living pest squatting in his gut. All she had done was prod him a little and check his temperature. Hardly what you would call a thorough examination.

"But what if the symptoms are delayed? Symptoms can be delayed, surely? Perhaps there's an incubation stage or something, before I start presenting. Aren't there some further tests you could do?"

Doctor Mulhindra pushed her glasses up her nose, staring down them at her patient. The look of annoyance on her face said more than her words.

"Mr Hinklow, I don't know how I can make this any clearer for you. You are not ill. You will not die from ingesting a fly, no matter what continent you may suppose it originated from. If it makes you feel any better, go home and take some multivitamins but I have other patients to see, patients with real problems, and I would be grateful if you would allow me the opportunity to give them the same time and courtesy as I have given you."

He got up and left. He didn't shake her hand. He never shook hands. As little physical contact as possible was for the best. You never knew what you would pick up.

~

He rolled it over in the Tupperware with one of the pencils he used for his crosswords. The pencil and tub would both have to be burned afterwards but he didn't see what other way he could do this with ease. His stool looked normal, or as normal as a lay person such as himself could tell. He was perfectly comfortable with his own lack of expertise. After all, what kind of fool makes a habit of examining the faeces of all manner of persons not knowing what kind of contagions might be festering within? Disgusting.

The stool was compact and moist, a long, brown sausage of discarded food, all sustenance and nutrition stripped from its being as his body had processed it from one end to the other. He rolled it over again, sticky brown residue clinging to the plastic. Nothing. He was expecting – no, hoping – to see a little nugget of black wedged within his defecation, almost raisin-like in appearance, but there was nothing. He slowly smushed up his poo with the end of his pencil, teeth marks indented in its veneer from hours of nervous nibbling, as he searched in vain for the fly. All that he was left with was a shit-covered pencil and a growing sense of dread. There was only one thing he could conclude. The fly was still inside him.

~

Even with the windows open his bedroom was still hot and close. He had read briefly before trying to get some rest. It had been a good hour or so before sleep finally claimed him yet when it did, it was anything but pleasant.

The dream started ordinarily enough, him lying there in the garden on his lounger reading a book of detective tales. They were the good old fashioned ones that he liked where the language was clean and the detectives well-educated. None of this violent stuff that seemed *de rigueur* nowadays. He had just put his book aside, reaching down beside him for a cold drink, when a buzzing sound distracted him. It was nothing at first, a subtle hum tainting the summer's breeze, little more than the noise of lawns being mown. It grew quickly, grabbing his attention, filling the air with a persistent drone. What had been a cloudless sky gradually darkened as the sun became hidden from view. Above him hovered a black cloud shimmering with a thousand bodies, multitudes of flies clustering together, their droning jarring his nerves as he stared at them, dumbstruck.

One by one they drifted down towards him. The first few he swatted away with his hand, before resorting to attacking them with his book in an effort to drive them back. A few became dozens, dozens became hundreds, hundreds became thousands, hoards of winged beasts forcing themselves upon him as he struggled to get away. Stumbling as he ran across the lawn, he found himself prone on his back, arms flailing in the air as they besieged him. They were everywhere, entering every orifice, climbing up his nostrils, crawling into his mouth, clambering inside his ears. All of them trying to force themselves inside him, desperate to get to the fly within him, choking him with their efforts.

He woke up with a start. In the darkness he could still hear the buzzing sound permeating throughout the room. The sound of tiny buzz saws darting around his head. His hands felt frantically for the lamp on his bedside table, knocking his book to the floor and taking his glasses with them. He didn't care. He could get them in a second. He just needed some light.

With a satisfying click the lamp flooded the room with light, sending the shadows scurrying to the corners. Even bleary-eyed with sleep he could see that there was no swarm of flies festooning his bedroom, no legion of disease clustering above his bed. If anyone could see him now...

With a degree of relief he scratched around on the floor for his spectacles. His fingertips finally brushed across the thin frames and he looped the wire stems around his ears. His bed sheets were dishevelled, thrown about during his dream. He pulled back what little cover remained there and shuffled over to the dresser. It had been his mother's. This was where he used to sit with her as a child when she would brush her hair, her face reflected in its mirror as he sat on her lap. It was too grand for his needs, truth be told, but that didn't matter to him. She had left it to him and it would stay with him until the day he died.

He peered deeply into the mirror, pulling back his nostrils and checking his ears. The sensation of insects quivering over his face still plagued him but there was nothing to be seen. The product of an overactive imagination, his mother would have said. All that was staring back at him was the tired face of a weary old man, hair thinning with wrinkles creasing his forehead. The only things sprouting from his orifices were the same old tufts of hair that had been there for as long as he could remember now.

"Silly old sod," he muttered to himself as he retraced his steps back to his bed. Even so, he felt queasy knowing that 'thing' was still crawling around inside him. Who knew what it was doing. What if it was female? Oh God, what if it was putting down eggs ready for a host of offspring to hatch in his guts? What would he do then?

Tomorrow. He would do something about it tomorrow. He could worry about it then. For now he needed sleep.

Easing himself back into bed he felt for the light switch once more, ready to brave the dark again. As his fingers fumbled along the cord for the button he found himself sitting stock still staring at the lamp.

There on the shade, silhouetted against the light, were three bulbous flies.

~

He went down the hardware store the very next day and bought up all their stocks of flypaper, aerosol repellents and swatters. It had cost him the best part of that week's pension but he didn't care. It wasn't enough that he had to deal with that disease carrying pest within him, now it was bringing in reinforcements, calling out to the rest of the shit eaters out there to come into his home with their infection spreading bodies.

It took him the best part of the morning to hang the papers from the ceiling. They dangled there in every room, hundreds of rolls of the stuff, sticky strips of death waiting to catch their intended victims. He had heard that mice would gnaw their own legs off to escape similar devices and wondered if a fly would do the same, vainly breaking off leg after leg in an attempt to free themselves.

Once all the papers were set he started work on the rest of the house. As well as the repellents he had bought heavy duty gaffer tape, thick black rolls of the stuff, more than enough for what he had in mind.

He went into each room armed with the tape and scissors, stopping at each window, door and crevice to unravel a good length of tape and stretch it across the seals. He was thorough, double taping every time, making sure that there wasn't enough space for even a silverfish to fit through let alone a fly. The fireplace was another matter entirely, the potential flaw in his plan. He blocked the flume with newspapers as best he could, praying it would suffice, and sealed the living room shut with tape. By the time he was done, every room was sealed bar three, and the house was airtight to the outside world. The only route he left for himself within the house was a run of open doors from his kitchen, through the hallway then upstairs to his bathroom and bed. All he could do was eat, shit and sleep, but that would be fine for now.

~

Sitting at his kitchen table, he waited. The first thing to do was stay healthy. He had to keep himself fighting fit throughout the process. Every hour, on the hour, he would take his pills. They were lined out in rows before him, small white plastic containers all with tiny childproof lids. He meticulously set out each tablet on the table top at the appointed time, little coloured spheres of health and vitality ready to enter his bloodstream. The first he popped were a host of multivitamins, a rainbow of colours sitting on his tongue. He washed these down with a cold glass of water and followed them swiftly with a dose of Echinacea and a couple of antibiotics. The labels said each pill should only be taken once every four hours but he didn't care. This was all out war and sometimes you had to break the rules.

The second course of action was attack. After each dose of pills was gone, he would swig a mouthful of cod liver oil straight from the bottle; the time for decorum long gone. The taste was vile, a combination of grease and fermented fish, enough to make his face screw up with each measure, but it was a hardship he would have to live with. If the fly wouldn't come out of its own accord then he was bloody well going to flush it out in a sea of his own effluence.

~

His first bowel movement took place shortly after lunch, brought on by the cod liver oil. He had made himself a crisp bacon, lettuce and tomato sandwich, the bread lightly toasted and covered with a generous helping of mayonnaise. He had gone to wash up and then realised something was awry. Staring up at him from the centre of the sink was the plug hole, five gaping ovals sitting in a neat circle eagerly waiting for a whole platoon of flies to emerge from the plumbing. He snapped the plug into place with as much haste as he could muster and put the plate swiftly to one side. If he had forgotten this one then what about the ones upstairs?

Weaving through the flypapers in the hallway, his own personal slalom course, he scurried up the stairs to the landing. It was then that his stomach growled.

'*Oh Christ,*' he thought, buttocks clenching as he felt his innards loosening.

Shuffling forwards, arms by his sides as he tugged his underwear free of his backside, he waddled along the corridor and into the bathroom like some kind of demented, giant penguin. Frantically he clawed at his belt, squirming on the spot as he fought the compulsion to shit where he was standing, where his still warm waste would run down his legs like overripe silage. The belt came loose and he struggled his trousers down around his ankles, a damp patch of sweat staining the back of his underwear as he foisted them free. With a deep sense of relief he collapsed onto the toilet and let nature take its course.

He repeated the process on four more occasions that day with the same result each time. And each time there was still no fly in sight.

~

His house was like a sauna. It had been one whole week since he had sealed himself in and the heat wave hadn't abated. He was weaker than he could ever remember. Some would say it was a combination of the self-induced diarrhoea, the heat and a lack of food. He knew better, that the disease-spreading cause was resting firmly in his gut.

The expectation had been that this would take a day to deal with, two at the most. Seven days in and supplies were running low. He couldn't go outside and get more, that would let the enemy in. He was certain that a whole swarm was hovering outside, waiting to get through to the tyrant within him.

He knew it was still alive inside him. He was positive of it. He could feel its dirty, hairy legs crawling around his stomach, its proboscis sucking at his insides. There were tiny twitches and twinges within his bowels as it flitted merrily along his internal passageways. Each miniature passing tickling the fleshy walls of his guts. And then there was the burrowing as she laid her eggs. That was what hurt the most. Sudden sharp pains from nowhere, cramping his innards and making him double over in agony. A doctor would have told him it was the hunger pangs kicking in, a combination of that and the dehydration brought on from his regular toilet trips. Oh yes, a doctor would tell you that. But what a doctor couldn't explain was the buzzing.

It had started a couple of days previously, sitting in his kitchen in the heat of the late afternoon. The room was stuffy as ever, the cloying scent of the hanging flypapers adding to his discomfort. All he wanted to do was sleep. Slumping forward, his arms folded on the table in front of him, he had put his head down. A quick forty winks. That would be fine. After all, what else did he have to do other than wait for nature to eventually take its course? As he settled, he yawned. Just a small one, his mouth barely open more than an inch or so. That was when he heard it.

Bzzz

His mouth clamped shut. He opened it again.

Bzzz

It went on like that over the next two days. Every time he opened his mouth the drone of tiny wings came forth, as if there was a microscopic vibrator pleasuring his throat.

It was at the end of that first day, though, that a new plan started forming in his mind. If he could hear the buzzing then there might be another way to cleanse his system. All he needed was a lure. Something to entice her to crawl back up the way she had entered.

The meat was ripe. He had plucked it from the overflowing kitchen bin, the sack filled with a week's worth of refuse and half-finished meals. When he had been able to eat he was only able to force a little bit down with each passing day. Most of it had gone to waste. This offering hadn't even seen the heat of the pan, a discarded piece of steak he had been too queasy to even contemplate. Now, after days of sitting in the heat, its ruddy flesh had become green in places, an oily sheen glistening on its surface, slimy to the touch. Normally the stench of decay would have been enough to make him gag, but needs must when the Devil drives.

He dissected the meat with a sharp knife, cutting it into neat, uniform cubes, each placed directly in front of him. The next part proved more difficult. It had taken several minutes of rummaging before he finally found what he was after in the back of a kitchen drawer. The string was long and thin, the kind used by butchers to wrap parcels of meat, perfect for his requirements. He cut several lengths, each a foot long, and diligently wrapped them round each chunk of meat. The work was fiddly, his aged fingers unused to this level of dexterity, slipping as they struggled with the individual knots. Eventually he was left with seven perfect parcels, all wrapped up and ready to go.

And so the trap was set. He held a lure above him, mouth open, head tipped back. Instantly he was hit by that buzzing sound. A monotonous drone. That was all for the good this time. That meant his quarry was ready. There for the taking.

He angled his head back further, opening his throat up like a sword swallower in an effort to clear the path for his lodger. He sat like that for hours, cramp seeping into his muscles but he didn't care. He was so close to victory. He was sure of it. That was all that mattered now. Luring the pest from within. He didn't even notice when he nibbled the first piece of meat as it hung there above him.

A heap of bloodied string lay piled on the table when he admitted defeat for the day and trudged upstairs to his bed.

~

He hummed to himself that evening as he drifted off to sleep. It was a simple tune, one from his childhood. Who would have thought it would prove so apt in later life. He wondered where on earth he might get a cat, dog, cow and horse at this time of night and then thought better of it. Maybe he should just start off with a spider to begin with and see where that got him. That's if he could live with the wriggly-jiggliness of it all.

He giggled to no one in particular.

~

The pain. Oh God, the pain. His insides were on fire.

He rolled out of bed and collapsed onto the floor, his knees hitting the floorboards hard.

That was when he vomited – vast swathes of fluid pouring out from him and splattering across the wooden floor.

"Holy Mary, mother of Christ," he muttered to himself as he crouched there on all fours, sweat dripping from his forehead.

Another cramp hit him in the guts and he doubled over onto the floor, rolling in his own filthy mess. He lay there on his back, staring at the ceiling in the early morning light, and that was when he saw them. Hundreds of spots floating before his eyes. Wildly diving around the room in flights of ecstasy.

"They got in. They bloody well got in."

He had to do something. He had to act now before they engulfed him in a wave of pestilence.

He staggered to his feet, slipping in his own vomit as he struggled from the room. Rolls of flypaper covered him as he thrashed his way out of the bedroom and down the hallway but he didn't care anymore.

His arms swung dementedly around his head, a whirling dervish recklessly swatting the air around him. Each swipe brought more flypaper down around his shoulders, fragrant orange strips sticking to his clothing as he fought his way into the kitchen. Still the spots swarmed around him, an incessant buzzing throbbing throughout his skull as they mocked him.

The cans were resting beside the sink where he had placed them, two litres of fly spray, enough insecticide for a whole army of flies the shopkeeper had joked with him. How little did he know how close to the truth he was.

He stood there, legs spread, arms outstretched as he drained the cans. He was the epitome of a small town sheriff in a cheap old western, guns drawn, ready to fight the good fight. A fine mist filled the air in front of him, the sickly odour mingling with the rest of the stench of the house as he pressed down on each canister. The floor became a sea of black as tiny bodies fell to the floor but they still kept coming. Carcasses squelched underfoot as he steadied himself against the perpetual onslaught, the tiled floor becoming slick with the fluids of the dead beneath his feet. He kept spraying, waiting for the last of them to die but it never happened. The empty canisters clattered on the floor as he flung them aside, hundreds more flies continually flooding the room.

And still they danced around the ceiling,

black specks infuriating him as they called out to their queen. And she was answering them. Calling out from his guts to her brood. 'Come join me,' she was saying. 'It's warm in here, we can feast for eternity and live like Gods.'

They dive bombed him, making for his face, his ears, his nose, his mouth. Others went south, searching for his anus.

The knife was in his hand before he knew it, instinct and madness taking hold simultaneously. The truth was there, it had been evident to him all along but he had never had the strength to admit it to himself until now. All this time he had been trying to entice her out, flush her out, just draw the goddamned fucking bitch out of his body. That was wrong. That was the fool's way. No, he had to take the front foot here. He had to man up. He had to go in after her.

He scurried under the heavy wooden table, the only barrier he could find between him and the flies. It wouldn't give him more than a few precious seconds but he prayed that would be enough. The tiles were hard beneath his back as he lay there prostrate. All around he could feel the agitation in the air as the swarm clambered for their queen. It was now or never, do or die.

Buttons flew in all directions as he ripped open his bed shirt with what little strength remained to him. His greying skin was taut against his body, his ribcage etching out a human xylophone across his sunken chest. The tip of the knife rested intimately against his abdomen, teasing the flesh with the delicacy of a surgeon. He could feel her writhing within him, calling out to her brethren, 'Stop the oppressor, stop him now before it's too late, before he steals the promised land from you all.' But it was too late. She had miscalculated and his was the victory. All he had to do was cut deep and cut steady and then she would be his.

They were upon him now. Flurrying around his face, desperate to get in, to suffocate, to annihilate, to venerate. A confusion of hatred and adoration as they swarmed the oppressor in desperation to be with their queen. He was stronger though, smarter, more obstinate. He clenched his jaw tight, even as they forced themselves up his nostrils, stifling his airways as he prepared himself. This was his moment, his victory, his salvation. This was when he claimed his life back. And that was when the blade bit deep.

With the first scream the flies flooded his body.

~

It was several weeks later that his body was found, after the neighbours complained of a terrible smell coming from the property. The police were called in as a matter of course, though death by suicide was the only real explanation following the autopsy. It took days to clean the place up and varying rumours were bandied around the area. What never made the papers was the manner in which they found the body. Something the coroner remarked upon as unique in his thirty-one years of practice. Never in that time had he seen a body which had decomposed from the inside out.

Virtually
Famous

He'd died a thousand times today and would die a thousand more, remembering little to nothing of what had passed previously. Each time he felt nothing and would continue to do so *ad infinitum*. He'd been chosen because of his fame and his looks. A chiselled jawline shadowed with the appropriate thickness of stubble. Blonde hair which defied the laws of gravity and held just so. And those piercing blue eyes which looked as if they had been crafted by the Devil himself. He wasn't perfect. He had habits. Ones frowned upon in polite society. Habits he kept hidden as best he could. The producers who had come calling didn't care about any of that other than to consider the media coverage his involvement would evoke. After all, a history of drink and drugs was to be expected, as were his rotational visits to rehab – a place it was suggested he would have a permanent room in one day.

From a young age, he became used to seeing his image wherever he went. It was inescapable. His smile lit up billboards across America when he was barely nine and he had been in and out of the magazines ever since he could remember. He grew up in front of the American public, going from babyfaced sweetheart to teenage heartthrob only to fall from grace before them too. And he fell hard. Harder than he thought was possible. He had regular fights with his parents in his late teens. The arguments were mainly over the money he was making for them and how little came his way. The tabloids lapped it up. The eventual 'divorce' from his parents was splashed across the front of every tittle-tattle rag and website in the country. That was the event which most commentators speculated to be the true catalyst for his subsequent problems. Directors stopped working with him in the years which followed as a chaotic reputation blossomed around him. He was reduced to walk-on parts on cable comedy shows or taking roles in low budget straight-to-DVD films. Invariably these ended up in the $1 bins within weeks of their release. Yet in the early part of his twenties he experienced a brief renaissance in his fortunes. A surprise hit science fiction movie revived interest in his career. This was followed by a spate of supporting roles in more high profile productions, with rumours abound he was in line for the next big blockbuster, only for his addictions to drag him down into the gutter once more. He was all but washed up for a second time before he'd even made it to his thirties.

It was no wonder he took the job when he received the call.

~

"Chet Tyler?"

Chet looked up from his magazine. The publication was a glossy affair which purported to expose the salacious truth of the celebrity world. It landed clumsily on the coffee table in the middle of the waiting room as he flung it to one side. Rising, he uncurled his body from the depths of his seat, a modern design full of impractical curves and soft cushioning. Other men sat in similar chairs, each of them struggling to hold on to their twenties. They were all of a type, a selection of clones, the sort which caused heads to turn and cameras to flash. If you squinted it became impossible to readily discern one from the other. Greens and reds played across their perfect cheekbones and blemish-free foreheads, flickering light spilling from flat screen monitors inserted into the surrounding walls. The Transgressive Games logo flashed up on each screen simultaneously as it had done on repeat for the thirty minutes Chet had been waiting. Images of people laughing and having fun followed the logo, folks drinking champagne and partying into the night, all shown through the eyes of an anonymous host. Chet ignored all of this and opened the narrow door to the subsequent room.

The room was almost barren, the walls white and devoid of decoration. Towards the rear was a desk of a style commonplace in the receptions of large corporate organisations. A woman sat positioned behind the desk, staring intently at the screen in front of her. A small headset was fixed over a bobbed haircut, the thin stem of the mouthpiece tight against her right cheek. Her lips moved as she engaged in conversation. Every now and then she tapped a manicured fingernail at the screen as if reassuring herself of the evidence of her argument.

Chet coughed.

The woman paused in her conversation, raising an eyebrow as she looked in his direction, her hand covering her mouthpiece.

"I heard my name over the speakers," he ventured, locking and unlocking his fingers, unsure of what to do with his hands as he stood waiting.

"Through there." Her extended arm indicated a secondary door to his right which he had not previously noticed. "He'll be waiting for you in there."

He went to ask her why she hadn't told him that when he stepped into the room. It was clear why he was there. And, after all, didn't she know who he was? Instead he said "Sure," and followed her direction.

Her conversation continued as the door shut behind him.

"Chet! How are you, buddy?" The accent was thick New Yorker. Chet's hand was pumped vigorously in a grip formed of sausage fingers draped with gold, his smaller hand dwarfed between two clam shells.

"Fine, I guess," said Chet. He looked down at the hands holding his. There was something he needed to remember about them. Something he couldn't quite recall.

"You sure? You don't look so great."

"Yeah, I'm good. I'm good." His voice belied his certainty. Chet glanced up from the hands and back at the man who had greeted him, taking in the room at the same time.

It was the size of a school gymnasium. The walls were painted black and led up to an innocuous ceiling set high above the ground. There was an absence of natural daylight throughout; each and every window was covered with dark heavy cloth. Illumination for the room bled down from mounted strip lighting positioned at regular intervals along the ceiling. A few chairs were scattered here and there across the floor, most of them standing upright. A cloth covered table was set up on the far side of the room with an array of paraphernalia decked out along its surface. Beyond that was a room within a room. A rectangle formed of weighted curtains hanging from a prefabricated shell. Oversized spotlights faced into the space like miniature suns burning brightly in the dark.

A single video camera stood staring into the canvas-screened room, mounted on a tripod and abandoned for now.

"Was it the wait? I guess it was the wait." A meaty hand slapped him on the back in apology. "Sorry, Chet, I had a few things to sort out in here."

"Are you seeing others today? I thought I was the only one."

"Others?"

"In the waiting area. The others there."

Chet's host dropped his smile momentarily, putting a hand to his face. He stroked his jawline as he studied Chet's features before reaching across and patting him on the shoulder.

"Don't worry about them, Chet. This is all about you." The hand dropped down Chet's arm and Chet felt a gentle tug on his elbow. "Let's go, shall we?"

Chet allowed himself to be guided, shuffling one foot in front of the other like a somnambulist. There was a familiarity to the building he couldn't ascribe. Perhaps it was the mundanity of the interior, the sparsity of detail confusing it with a multitude of other studios he had been inside. He simply couldn't tell why but he knew it was important.

The items on the trestle table were more apparent as they ventured closer toward the camera. They reminded Chet of props he had used on a short lived gangster serial. He had been the hero, a smart-mouthed cop who invariably blurred the lines between legality and anarchy. Only three episodes had aired before the network pulled the plug. He didn't care. He had blown his money from the show on a month long ingestion of amphetamines and alcohol as he partied with a medley of people whose faces he could not remember.

"Have I been here before?" he asked.

His guide turned to look Chet in the face.

"You don't remember?"

Chet remained silent, taking in the barren architecture. "You once told me this is where The Game was born," his host continued. "This was where it all began. Out here in the middle of nowhere."

"The Game?" queried Chet, rolling the words over his tongue, testing the power of the syllables out loud. "The Game?"

"Yes, Chet. The motherfucking Game." The man opposite sighed. His face loomed closer to Chet's, peering inquisitively into his eyes. "Jeez, how much stuff did you take this time?"

"This time?" Chet took a step back, creating distance between the pair of them, his eyes refocusing on the rotund face which seemed so full of queries.

"Don't worry about it, kid." Those sausage fingers again, this time patting his cheek, leaving a sheen of grease on Chet's face. "Let's get on with this, shall we?"

~

The Game.

It had been a smash hit. A billion dollar success. Sold out in all territories across the globe. People could not get enough. Employees found themselves fired from their jobs whilst lost within The Game. Rumours abounded that people had even died during gameplay from malnutrition, something the media had been happy to hype. And the developers milked it for everything it was worth. The more warnings they slapped on The Game the more people wanted to buy it. Within the first year it was estimated over sixty-five percent of the US population had played The Game at one time or another. And Chet was the face of it. His journey back to stardom was complete.

The rise of virtual reality and the public's obsession with celebrity and riches had created the perfect storm. The Game captured the zeitgeist, riding the wave of desire and jealousy with consummate ease. It dragged the fame-hungry into a world of luxury and decadence, things most had only been able to dream of before. Of course it hadn't been called The Game in its infancy. Back then it had carried Chet's name but that had changed as The Game evolved. Chet's World had been a place for people to be Chet. It was their chance to escape into celebrity culture in a way the magazines, reality shows and PR-operated social media accounts could never hope to match. Within seconds of jacking into The Game you were Chet. Living and breathing his life. A synthesised existence updated with new storylines every single day. The coding was exquisite. The experience sublime. Everything was based on Chet's life, all of it filmed twenty-four hours previously over a morning or afternoon before being uploaded to the system. An integrated artificial intelligence filled in the rest, developing multiple outcomes based on the real life footage. A million variations all from one common source. Reality blurred with fiction. Truth became meaningless. Interpretation redundant. Experience everything.

Over time Chet's World changed, morphing into something unexpected, becoming something new with one simple edict. One which appealed to the base nature of its fandom. One attuned to the seething cocktail of envy and aggression. One which had the simplest of resolutions. The Game became how to kill Chet Tyler.

No one was ever truly able to pinpoint the moment of transition. Theories were rife among social commentators, vloggers and technology experts. Some suggested rogue hackers had engineered a backdoor into the system. Others hypothesised this had always been the end game for the developers, a way to create an addiction and then feed the public with more hardcore storylines as their need for a stronger fix grew. The most common conjecture described a scenario where the system's artificial intelligence had simply responded to the needs of the audience.

Chet's World, or The Game as it became, had

always allowed people to play as any number of characters. Friends could jack in as part of a multiplayer package, appearing as members of Chet's entourage or as random fans desperate to get his autograph and maybe something a little more salacious.

However, in the beginning it was only the minority who played this way. The majority wanted to be Chet and experience fame first hand, to sip from the Devil's cup so to speak. A not insubstantial number of players ended up in therapy convinced they were Chet Tyler after being immersed in The Game for far too long.

What no one knew until much later was that the only person who knew exactly what it was like to be Chet Tyler was a player of The Game too.

At first Chet had watched remotely. There were any amount of internet channels where he could view gamers waxing lyrical about their online actions as they simulcast their immersion in The Game. It had been a novelty initially. An amusing way to pass time between shoots. A half hour here or an hour snatched there. His viewing time increased as the months wore on. Mild vanity gradually turned to addiction without his realising, even as Chet's World evolved. The first time he saw himself die he was lying in his own bed, silk sheets covering his legs and groin, his chest exposed to the world. He was halfway between sleep and consciousness with only his own narcissism keeping his eyes from closing. The onscreen point of view had been that of a fan's as they approached him at a signing for his autobiography; ghostwritten by a writer he had only ever spoken to by phone. Chet never saw the gun which shot him. The weapon was off-camera, held too low, and fired from the shooter's hip. All he saw was the reaction on his face as the bullet bit deep into his chest followed by a flower of crimson spreading across the white landscape of his immaculately presented shirt. Chet's hands had instinctively clutched to his chest in real life, grasping at the spot inches beneath his clavicle where the bullet had entered his virtual body. He had watched himself die in films a hundred times before but this was different. This time his death was more personal, more grounded in reality. Chet swallowed desperate gulps of air as his brain struggled to process the images on screen. His fingers went from his chest to the covers, his body forming a crucifix as he grasped for purchase as his whole world collapsed around him. It was only when the adrenaline kicked in that he was able to regain composure. After that it became a new addiction for him. Another hit for an old time junkie. He sought out the videos of his online demise. The darker the better. There was an elaborateness in some of his deaths which continued to surprise him over and over again. The only limit was the imagination of the gamer. Sometimes people took it to a whole new level, torturing him for hours on end before either his body gave out or the perpetrator's own levels of boredom prompted them to resolve the situation. And all the time the download figures for the clips continued climbing up and up and up.

He remembered the faces of all those who'd killed him in The Game: a red-faced double-chinned man in a navy business suit; another heavily bearded, with a distinctive port-wine birth mark on his face. A nurse, two women who looked like sisters. A blank-faced man with a bald head getting out from behind the wheel of a taxi with a gun in his hand; a woman in a long black nightdress stepping from a hotel room wielding silver scissors, her bare feet bloodied. Even a young girl, once, a thin broomstick of a thing, bruised knees and grubby palms.

He remembered their faces from The Game. At least, that's where he hoped he remembered them from.

~

Chet and his host approached the video camera within the curtained area. One foot placed after another, after another, after another, the sound of their footsteps hollow in the vastness of the room. Chet stopped. He could feel a tackiness clutching at the soles of his sneakers. He imagined warm gum on the sidewalk softened by the heat of the midday sun but the pull was subtler than that. He looked to his feet. The outline of an irregular patch of darkness was partially visible against the black texture of the flooring. Other footsteps had corrupted the mark and overlaid it with dirt from the soles of their shoes. Chet crouched down. He dragged his finger along the ground feeling a mixture of grit and something which resembled semi-dried syrup. Strawberry perhaps. He lifted his finger to see what it was.

Chet paused. His companion was standing by the curtains. His portly physique silhouetted in the blaze of light behind him as if in homage to Hitchcock on those old TV shows Chet's dad made him watch as a kid. Hitch was shouting words at Chet. Trying to get his attention.

"Chet. I need you here, Chet. I need to know if this was you. I really need to know if this was you."

~

Would it be murder or suicide? It was a question he asked himself innumerable times before he finally took the plunge.

There had been failed attempts where he geared himself up for the deed only to relent at the last minute. He likened it in his mind to inserting a needle into your own veins. The fear of the pain was always greater than the reality. One moment of discomfort followed by hours of reward and ecstasy.

He had chosen pills in the end. Ground up and mixed with a cocktail of Jägermeister, schnapps and honey liqueur to disguise the taste. It was meant to be a kindness. A way for faux-Chet to drift off into the electronic nether with the minimum of pain. It was the way he would want to go himself when the time came. He had not anticipated the vomiting and the pleading. Slender fingers had grasped at his avatar's trouser leg, gripping the fabric for dear life. Chet had watched his own face staring up at him imploringly, begging for help, blood flecked saliva foaming on lips he had used for the most intimate of pastimes. Hands belonging to his character pushed faux-Chet away, leaving the virtual him to whimper on the floor in a nauseating pool of its own stomach fluids. Five minutes of listening to the agonised mewling had been enough. He had acted without thinking. Grabbing the nearest thing to hand. Repeatedly bludgeoning the bottle of spirits into faux-Chet's skull. Over and over and over again. Playing a perverse game of whack-a-mole with only one target and with the strokes meeting less resistance as the pulpy mass on the floor increased.

It was a month before he tried again. This time he used a gun. He assumed the role of one of his entourage to get close to faux-Chet, taking the shot from behind. The nose of the gun had nestled into faux-Chet's thick blonde hair, singeing the locks with the flare from the muzzle. This way he didn't have to look himself in the eyes as he did it. This way he could remind himself it was all still part of a game. A harmless, non-deadly game. By the end of that week he had killed himself twenty-seven more times.

He experimented. He took inspiration from the videos posted by other gamers. People he regarded as artists pushing boundaries. He found new weapons of choice. After all, he had nothing but time on his hands. By now he was a recluse. He had quit the prerecording shoots which fed the system. The developers hadn't cared. It saved them an unnecessary overhead, leaving the gameplay to be completely generated by the inbuilt AI. Chet had cited the risks to his wellbeing of filming any more scenes and that, in part, had been true. It had become too dangerous for Chet to live his normal life, whatever normal meant in that context. Stalkers had increased dramatically in line with the rise in sales of The Game. So he simply stayed in his room watching videos and jacking into The Game while spending a fortune on deliveries and home security. It was when the cutting started that things became worse.

~

Chet stood up.

"Chet, I need to know if this was you."

Chet licked his finger absentmindedly, ignoring the rasp of grit on his tongue. Whatever it was, it didn't taste like strawberry syrup. He ignored the pull at his sneakers as he walked to the curtained area.

"Chet, are you with me, buddy?" Two finger clicks sounded off in front of his face. "Chet, I need to know if you're in the room."

Chet blinked twice. His nostrils flared, inhaling deeply as he took in the scene.

"This wasn't me," he muttered, throwing his hands up to the sides of his temples. "This wasn't me."

He stumbled backwards, rushing from the curtained area, his legs rotating unnaturally beneath him as he lost his balance. He fell partly on the floor and partly into the props table, his head connecting with the cloth-covered edge. His fingers grasped at the cheap fabric, pulling it down level with him as he tried to claw his way to standing. Scalpels, gougers, chisels, hammers and blades of varying lengths clattered on the surrounding ground. A knife missed his splayed fingers as it fell point first to the floor. It stood upright with the tip held fast. Chet looked at the fallen blade with part of it reflecting the artificial light and the other part coated with a substance he knew did not taste of strawberry syrup.

~

"Which one is me? Which one is me? Which one is me?"

It was a mantra Chet rocked himself to sleep with, his arms wrapped around his knees as he sat up in bed.

"Which one is me? Which one is me? Which one is me?" The repetition was soothing, muttered with the insistent rhythm of a commuter train at full throttle.

"Which one is me? Which one is me? Which one is me?"

Exhaustion would claim him eventually. It always did.

His dreams were the same as his new reality, the one he lived online. In them he would be watching Chet Tyler but he was never sure if it was faux-Chet or himself. He had a scalpel in his dreams, a small one, the same as the clinicians used in the cosmetic surgeries dotted across the Hollywood hills. Chet or faux-Chet or whoever the fuck it was would always be compliant, sitting in a docile manner staring into the nothingness of the world, waiting for the inevitable to happen. There was a nonchalant swagger as he approached, scalpel in hand, a smile on his face, at ease with the inevitability of what was about to happen. He would sit astride their lap and pretend he was looking into the mirror as the cutting began, his muscles knotting and relaxing as he fought to keep the visage intact while the knife cut away the connecting tissue. He needed to see what lay beneath the façade. He needed to know if the real Chet was in there or if the real Chet was really still him.

He woke early with the deaths from his dreams echoing inside his head. A xylophone of ribs stood prominent beneath his skin as he sat naked on the oversized bed. The jack slid easily into his neck, the sensation familiar and reassuring like slipping into conversation with an old friend. It took less than a second for him to be ported into his other reality. The welcome point blinked into view as the system took over his neural indicators.

"Good morning," the system announced. Chet watched the woman seated behind the desk as she spoke. "Who would you like to be today?"

"Vinny. I'd like to be Vinny today."

"Of course. Please go through there. They'll be expecting you."

His fingers locked and unlocked as he stood waiting. An effervescent tingle passed momentarily from his scalp down to his toes. The experience was always the same as the AI adjusted the player's avatar. He knew what he would see if he looked in a mirror. He had worn this person so many times before. Killed himself a hundred times from inside this body. He'd see the chubby hands. The gold jewellery. The slight roll of neck flab. The receding hairline hovering above a thin slick of sweat. A perfect simulation of Chet's manager.

Chet stepped through the door on the far side of the room.

~

"Chet, you need to answer me. This one is too close to home."

Chet looked from the knife to Vinny.

Vinny wearily ran a hand across his face. He exhaled in a controlled manner, long and slow, scrunching his eyes shut as he pinched the bridge of his nose. He let his hand drop and spoke to Chet as if he were a parent talking to a child.

"Chet, it's the meds. I know it's the meds. Everything's going to be fine." He edged two steps towards his client with hands raised in what he hoped would be a placating manner.

"Stay away from me, Vinny. I'm warning you."

Vinny checked his progress. Chet was moving, using the upturned table for purchase to enable him to stand. The knife was no longer visible on the floor.

"Chet? What are you doing, Chet?"

Chet's legs quivered as he steadied his stance. The knife was in plain sight now, held firmly out in front of him.

"Don't mess with me, Chet. Not now. Not today. We've a small window of opportunity to make this go away but I need the truth."

"I'm not the one who is lying!"

"Listen, if it wasn't for me you would be sitting in a cell right this fucking minute."

"You're lying!"

"I followed you, Chet. I came all the way out here to the middle of nowhere just to make sure you were fine. And this was what I found." Vinny spread his arms wide, indicating the curtained scene behind him. "Chet, there's a man's body lying in there with its goddamned motherfucking face cut off! Now I need you to tell me if that was you and then I can deal with it."

"Of course it wasn't me!"

"Then who was it! You got in a car, the pair of you, and drove out here. Jeez, did you film it, Chet? Is that what the camera's for?"

"Drove with who?"

"You and your latest beau. Harold was it?" Vinny snorted a laugh. "I bet you didn't even know his name."

"I don't know anyone called..." Chet stopped. "Wait. Wait. They'll tell you."

"Who, Chet? Who will tell me?"

"The lady in the reception, the others in the waiting room. They'll tell you I've been waiting here for ages. I couldn't have done it."

A look of pity crossed Vinny's face.

"There is no reception, Chet. Just this hangar of a studio. If you don't believe me go see for yourself. Go on. The door's right there."

Chet's eyes followed the direction Vinny was pointing in, back to where he had entered the room.

"I found you passed out in the corner when I got here, Chet."

Chet ignored him and strode for the exit.

"You were lying right over there."

The door was feet away. Five steps and he would be there.

Four.

Three.

"Don't go through there, Chet. You don't want to go through that door." Vinny's voice rose louder the further Chet got from him. "You won't like what you see."

Two.

"Chet!"

One.

Chet's hand grasped the handle and the door swung open.

"I told you, Chet. I warned you. You wouldn't listen to me."

Chet clutched at the doorjamb with his free hand, looking out into the sandy terrain spread out before him. Two cars sat parked outside.

"I don't understand. They were there. There

was a room... and a desk... and a woman. They were real."

Vinny's footsteps sounded behind him, coming closer.

"The others in the waiting room, they were watching the screens. There was a reality show playing. No wait. It was a game. A game was playing."

"There was no room, Chet. There was no game."

Chet started to chuckle, letting the knife hang limp in his grip.

"What are you laughing at, Chet? I don't get it. What's so goddamned funny?"

"I remember. I remember now. You said it when I got here. This is where The Game started. We're in The Game." Chet's eyes sparkled with withheld tears. "All this time we've been in The Game."

"There is no Game, Chet. You're the one who always told me about The Game. You made it up. Try to remember, Chet. It's the meds messing with your head. Making up things which don't exist. Don't you remember anything?"

"We're in The Game, Vinny." Chet's words were more assured. "That's it, Vinny. You're just a collection of pixels. It's as simple as that. All I have to say is two words."

"Don't do it, Chet."

"You can't stop me. Don't you get it, no one can stop me."

"Chet, I'm warning you. You don't want to do it."

"Game over, game over," shouted Chet, arms spread as if performing to a crowd.

Vinny waited, watching.

"Game over."

Nothing changed. Chet looked inside and outside the room, spinning in a circle, looking for an exit point to reality.

"I said 'Game over'!"

"Shouting's not going to change anything, Chet."

Chet dropped to his knees, clawing at the back of his neck as he hit the floor, grasping for the jack point which existed in real life.

"I tried to tell you, kid. It was all in your head. The doctors confirmed it. You must remember that."

Vinny crouched beside Chet, sighing gently as he took the bulk of his weight on his knees. He put a paternal hand on Chet's brow. Spittle and air bubbles formed on Chet's lips as he repeated his failed litany in an attempt to exit the system.

"This is what happened, Chet." Vinny's words were quiet and calm. "You lured Harold here with promises of who knows what. Maybe you were going to make him famous or maybe it was sex and drugs. Either way, that's his blood on the floor. That's his corpse inside the curtains with his pretty young face on the ground beside him."

"That's not true," spluttered Chet.

Vinny ignored him.

"You took that knife in your hand and used it on him. You had to know what was underneath. Whether it was you or not. It's not the first time, Chet. That's why the doctors had you on the meds. But it's got to stop now. It can't continue any more."

"Bullshit, Vinny. Bullshit. It was you. It's always you."

Tears were streaming down Chet's cheeks, his words slurred between a mixture of snot and confusion.

"Now, Chet, we both know that's not true."

"It is true. It was you."

Vinny stroked Chet's hair, calming an upset child. His right hand disappeared into his jacket pocket feeling for the reassuring weight of the gun inside.

"Don't worry, Chet. It will soon be alright. Uncle Vinny is going to make this go away just like he always does."

~

The woman sat behind the desk revealing perfect teeth within a perfect smile. The smile never faltered as the man entered the room. He was in his late twenties sporting a face which caused heads to turn and cameras to flash.

He stood waiting patiently for her to speak, his hands held together, his fingers locking and unlocking with a mild sense of anticipation, ready for what was to come.

"Good morning," she said. "Who would you like to be today?"

Also by Phil Sloman:

Novellas
Becoming David (Hersham Horror Books, 2016)

Visit Phil Sloman at his website:
insearchofperdition.blogspot.co.uk

blackshuckbooks.co.uk/shadows

Printed in Great Britain
by Amazon

43554149R00096